Benjamin Constant

ADOLPHE

TRANSLATED WITH AN INTRODUCTION
BY L. W. TANCOCK

PENGUIN BOOKS
BALTIMORE · MARYLAND

Penguin Books Ltd, Harmondsworth, Middlesex
U.S.A.: Penguin Books Inc., 3300 Clipper Mill Road, Baltimore 11, Md
AUSTRALIA: Penguin Books Pty Ltd, 762 Whitehorse Road,
Mitcham, Victoria

—

First published 1816
This translation first published 1964

—

This translation copyright © L. W. Tancock, 1964

Made and printed in Great Britain
by C. Nicholls & Company Ltd
Set in Linotype Granjon

CONTENTS

INTRODUCTION

I

THE French are a self-consciously intellectual race; they have a horror of the unexplained, they must know where they stand, and why. That is why they are penetrating critics, of themselves as well as of others, and unsatisfactory politicians, for politics are not rational, but empirical and opportunist. It is also why the most typical works of French literature are works which plumb the depths of the human character, its passions, its motives, and expose the myriad shifts and disguises of its self-centredness. Whether it be Montaigne, La Rochefoucauld, or Gide, clear self-knowledge is the aim. And because that is more important than anything else, the characteristic French masterpiece (though of course the discursive Montaigne is an exception) is economical in form, avoiding all by-products or dawdling by the wayside, all merely picturesque effects, all 'poetic' flights put in for their own sake.

A uniquely French expression of this ideal is the small, economical novel of uncompromising analysis of character and motive, usually autobiographical, usually dealing with a tragic love-affair, tragic because the stark facts of human nature cannot logically be worked out and death must be called in to end an impossible situation. Everything not bearing upon the main problem is ruthlessly pruned, and the result is a microcosm of the human condition. Some or all of these characteristics may be found in the miniature masterpieces which are not the least gift of France to the literature of the modern world: *Manon Lescaut, René, Adolphe, La Confession d'un enfant du siècle, Dominique,*

La Porte étroite, La Symphonie pastorale, are only a few examples.

Such works of fiction, often very thinly disguised autobiographies, are touchstones which reveal to which of two groups a critic, university lecturer, or writer of a doctoral thesis belongs. Which group is sheep and which goats is of course a matter of opinion. The 'scholars' comb libraries, manuscripts, parish registers, and suchlike in an endless checking of the text against the biographical facts. The 'aesthetes' are really only concerned with the creative processes of the artist who has utilized the purely personal and local as material to transmute into universal truth, recognizable by every reader as his own actual or potential experience, his own instincts and character. These ask themselves what possible object can be achieved by niggling about names, places, and dates, while the 'scholars', of course, dismiss the 'aesthetes' as quite unscientific generalizers, purely subjective essayists.

The case of Benjamin Constant and *Adolphe* has occupied scholars and aesthetes alike for a century and a half. But the story should be a lesson in humility for the omniscient scholars and in respect for science and documents on the part of the vague aesthetes. Benjamin set out precise, detailed information about himself in three texts, apart from *Adolphe*, none of which was available until many years after his death and two not until very recently. The first, known as *Le Cahier rouge*, simply because the manuscript is in a red notebook, is a frankly autobiographical fragment of which the real title is *Ma Vie*, and which sets out Benjamin's life from his birth in 1767 until 1787. This notebook passed, after the death of Benjamin's widow, through the hands of various members of the Constant family, and was not published until 1907. The second, *Cécile*, probably written in

1811, had an even more delayed appearance. Benjamin led such a nomadic life that boxes of his papers were deposited here and there for years, and it seems probable that the manuscript of *Cécile* was left in Germany from 1813 until 1826, when he had his things moved to Lausanne. After his death in 1830 this manuscript passed with other papers into the possession of relatives, and it was not available for publication until 1951. *Cécile* is an account, with names transparently disguised, of Benjamin's long and frequently interrupted courtship, if such it can be called, of Charlotte von Hardenburg, whom he met in 1793 but was not to marry, and then only secretly, until fifteen years later. The third vital text is the *Journal intime*, which was only known in a truncated and bowdlerized text until the real, unexpurgated one was published, with the family's permission, by Alfred Roulin in 1952.

2

Here, from the above sources, as well as from what was publicly known in his lifetime, are the facts of the first forty years of Benjamin Constant's life, to the time of his writing *Adolphe*:

Born on 25 October 1767, at Lausanne, the son of Juste Constant de Rebecque, a professional soldier in the service of the United Provinces of the Netherlands, Benjamin lost his mother, whose first child he was, a few days after his birth. The Constant family had ramified for generations along the northern shores of the Lake of Geneva, and belonged to the well-to-do cosmopolitan Swiss class who filled higher military and professional positions all over Western Europe. Benjamin's father, shy, distant, sarcastic, and not a little eccentric, left the upbringing of his only son to a series of incompetent, cranky, and sometimes vicious and even criminal tutors of various nationalities, whom he took on or discharged for no better reason than because he liked the look of them or had grown tired of them. One of these tutors, a Mr May, was taken on when Juste and his thirteen-year-old boy visited Oxford in 1781. Mr May and Benjamin travelled for some eighteen months together in Europe, but as from the outset Juste had encouraged his son to poke fun at his tutor, the educational value of the latter, apart from providing practice in spoken English, was not great. All the time the intellectual precocity of the boy, though undisciplined, was being nourished upon a diet of mixed reading, from works on history, religion, and philosophy to pornography, for indeed he had little else to do. In 1782, when he was under fifteen, he was entered as a student at the University of Erlangen, but by then his sexual precocity was as evident as his intellectual power, and he chose to scandalize the not easily scandalized society of eighteenth-century Germany by parading a 'mistress' of notoriously easy virtue, and he was recalled to Brussels by his father in May 1783. Juste's next idea was to send the boy to Edinburgh, where he arrived in July and where he spent, as a student in the University, the two happiest and most profitable years of his youth, making many lasting friendships and cutting a brilliant figure in the Speculative Society, but also gambling heavily. He finally had to be removed because of his debts. Two sojourns in Paris between 1785 and 1787 as pupil of the distinguished critic Suard were punctuated by bouts of calf love for older women and less innocent affairs with mercenary ones. It was during these Paris days that he made the acquaintance of Mme de Charrière, the first great influence upon his life.

Mme de Charrière, *née* van Zuylen (1740–1805), also known as Belle de Zuylen, was born and brought up in Holland and had married, in 1771, a Swiss gentleman who was then acting as mathematical tutor to her younger brother. She settled in her husband's home at Colombier, near Neuchâtel, and after some ten years of boredom with her kind and attentive but uninteresting husband, sought distraction in literary work. She achieved a certain fame, notably with her *Caliste* (1785), after the publication of which her husband brought her to Paris in search of a cure for her chronic depression. When they met in Paris Benjamin was nineteen and she forty-six. The relationship was what might be expected. The motherless, precocious youth found in this clever, unhappy, childless woman not only a substitute for a mother, but the first person with a mind equal to his own on which he could sharpen his wits. She not only held all ordinary people in scorn, but hated all prejudice, humbug, and artificial attitudes, demanding absolute honesty with oneself. *Pas de phrases* was what each asked of the other. Their endless talks did not improve Benjamin's character or way of looking at life, but they cleared his mind of cant and infinitely sharpened his self-knowledge and power of clear psychological analysis. The relationship was to continue on and off, including long stays at Colombier, through all the storms of Benjamin's life for nearly twenty years, until her death at the end of 1805. She, of course, is the old woman to whose death *Adolphe* refers in the first chapter of the novel.

Summoned to return to his father in the early summer of 1787, Benjamin ran away from Paris and spent the summer months in almost penniless wanderings in England and Scotland, begging and borrowing from various former student friends of the Edinburgh days. At twenty, rootless, cosmopolitan, speaking three languages, he was already an inveterate gambler and womanizer, but also of an extremely studious nature, already deeply interested in the philosophy and comparative religion which he was to regard as his main work throughout his life, and never more happy than when he was researching in a library.

All this is narrated in *Le Cahier rouge*. In 1788 Benjamin took up his first position, that of gentleman-in-ordinary to the Duke of Brunswick, and at Brunswick, in 1789, he married Wilhelmina (Minna) von Cramm. It was a foolish marriage, destined to failure from the start. Minna was older than he, shrewish and soon unfaithful, and by 1792 all was over except the final formality of divorce, which came three years later. But meanwhile, in 1793, he had met Charlotte von Marenholz (*née* von Hardenburg), who was most unhappily married to a much older man who was her own sister's lover. The long, chequered love story of Benjamin and Charlotte, which was to drag on for some fifteen years until their marriage, celebrated in absolute secrecy for fear of Mme de Staël, is told in *Cécile*.

It was apparently on the road between Nyon and Coppet, in September 1794, that Benjamin Constant met his doom. She is described, as Mme de Malbée, in *Cécile*:

When I met Mme de Malbée she was in her twenty-seventh year. Short rather than tall, and too full in the figure to be elegant, her features were irregular and too prominent and her complexion indifferent; she had the loveliest eyes in the world, very fine arms, hands on the large side but dazzlingly white, a magnificent bosom, quick, jerky movements, over-masculine attitudes, a very sweet voice which, when she was excited, had a singularly touching break in it – altogether a general effect which struck one unfavourably at first glance, but which, when Mme de Malbée spoke and grew animated, became irresistibly attractive. Her intellect, the most far-ranging that has ever belonged to any woman, and possibly to any man either, had, in serious discussion, more force than grace, and in what touched the emotional life, a hint of sentientiousness and affectation. But in her gaiety there was a certain indefinable charm, a kind of childlike friendliness which captivated the heart and established for the moment a complete intimacy between her and whoever she was talking to.... [translation mine]

Germaine de Staël, daughter and heiress of the wealthy financier-statesman Necker, was indeed the most brilliant and influential woman in Europe. She was also the most possessive and exhausting, a terror to friend and foe alike. Her restless existence was centred upon her father's château at Coppet, on the Lake of Geneva, which became not only a literary factory but the storm centre of the liberal intellectual resistance to the despotism of Napoleon. In politics she represented the disappointment of eighteenth-century progressive enlightenment when the Revolution, hailed at first as the culmination of all that men of good will had worked, written, and longed for, turned, as most revolutions do, into a ruthless, immoral tyranny. In literature she was the formulator, in her two great works of criticism *De la Littérature* (1800) and *De l'Allemagne* (1810), of Romanticism as a more or less coherent doctrine, from which manifestoes later theorists, such as Stendhal and Victor Hugo, took many ideas without acknowledgement. Her novels, *Delphine* (1802) and *Corinne* (1807) portraying heroines (herself) of outstanding intellect doomed to love men unworthy of them, though almost unreadable today were sensationally successful at the time. For years at Coppet and elsewhere during her wanderings, she had about her a court of clever men including Bonstetten, Sismondi, the brothers Schlegel, Barante, and Constant, and one woman, her intimate friend, Mme Récamier, the most beautiful woman in Europe, who now and then turned the head of one or other of the men just for her own amusement, but who was cold as ice and only really interested in her own virginal loveliness.

For years Benjamin was caught up in this extraordinary household. Life at Coppet was governed by the moods and caprices of its mistress. Meals were at any time, Mme de Staël swept unannounced into anybody's room at all hours of the day or night, wearing her crimson and emerald green turban and twirling a sprig of some evergreen shrub (the gardener cut them specially each day) in order to show off her hand and arm, and she talked for hours on end, usually about some idea she was developing in her current book. Nobody was allowed any personal life of his own, and she immediately dealt with any sign of rebellion by turning on the full pressure of her remarkable histrionic gifts, with weepings, screams, swoonings, and hysterics. At first Benjamin was captivated, not only by the woman's wonderful brain and irresistible personality, but also as a lover in the full sense of the word, following the select band of distinguished men, including Talleyrand, who had already passed that way. It is probable that Mme de Staël's next child, Albertine de Staël, born in 1797, was his. Not that all the time was spent in love-making, scenes, and play-acting, for together they worked at their writing (nothing ever stopped her writing), and while she was working on her books he was producing some remarkable political pamphlets and putting in time at his hobby and life work, the history of comparative religions.

Such intensity could not be maintained by an ordinary man, especially when Germaine's tyranny became more and more imperious. She would allow Benjamin leave of absence only on condition that he return at a stated time, she would demand to read his letters, she was not above making scenes in public, and if he overstayed a leave of absence she would drive in her grand coach to where he was and bring him back. Humiliations would be followed by passionate reconciliations, and always Benjamin's moral cowardice and genuine affection and pity would prevent him from making the break he constantly swore to himself to delay no longer.

A chance came in the late autumn of 1800. While temporarily alone in Paris Benjamin met in the salon of his good friend Mme Talma, wife of the great actor, a woman about five years older than himself, known as Anna Lindsay. Anna was the daughter of an Irish innkeeper of Calais, named O'Dwyer, but, having as a child charmed the Duchesse de Fitz-James, a guest at the inn, she had been brought up amid Parisian airs and graces. At about sixteen she had left the Duchess, been 'protected' by various gentlemen, and had eventually become, in 1789, mistress of M. de Lamoignon, by whom she had had two children and with whom she had been living for eleven years. When she met Benjamin she was thirty-eight and he thirty-three. The affair blazed up at once into a passionate attachment and followed a familiar pattern. Poor Anna fell genuinely in love with Benjamin and was prepared to leave her lover and children to marry him, but he, the chase having ended with capture of the prey, immediately took fright at becoming too involved and began to cool, the process being accelerated when things became dangerous owing to the arrival in Paris not only of M. de Lamoignon but also of Mme de Staël. By May 1801 Anna had left Paris, broken-hearted, and Germaine resumed her sway, soon asserting her authority by taking him with her for a protracted tour of Germany in search of material for her projected book on German thought and literature. There Mme de Staël terrified everybody by her merciless interrogations. The story is told that at Weimar, Goethe was so worn out that he decided to take to his bed with a diplomatic illness from which he did not recover until sure that she had left the town. However that may be, Benjamin Constant seems to have been a success with the great man.

Yet another chance of escape came in the spring of 1804, when Mme de Staël passed on her triumphal way from Weimar to Berlin and Benjamin went back alone to Lausanne. But this time it was his character that brought him back to her. He arrived at Lausanne on the 7th of April, and on the 9th, Necker, Germaine's father, died at Coppet. Immediately Benjamin was overcome with pity and anxiety and left at once for Germany to comfort Germaine in her grief and loneliness. He was more firmly tied than ever.

And so the situation dragged on. His diary records more and more appalling scenes, more and more vows to break with the tyrant, more and more cowardly surrenders. And then, out of the blue, Charlotte came back into his life. They saw each other at the end of 1804 after eleven years of separation. She had divorced Marenholz and married again in 1798, her second husband being a Frenchman, M. du Tertre. The revival of this old love after all these years turned the stormy, uncomfortable existence with Mme de Staël into an intolerable hell. In October 1806 he was with Mme de Staël at Rouen. On the 18th he left for Paris. The following extracts from the *Journal intime* tell the story and show up Benjamin's peculiar blend of passion and cold-blooded analysis (in the numerical code 1 = sexual pleasure, 12 = love for Charlotte):

19th. ... visited Mme du Tertre. She is much improved in looks. I think I have begun to make my meaning clear. If so, we are well away for 12. Dined with Prosper [de Barante]. I mean this evening to go as far as possible with Charlotte. I will write down the result tomorrow. *Wrote this evening to Mme de Staël* [italics Constant's].

20th. Charlotte has yielded. Consequently 1. Afterwards I did what I could to calm her. Hope I have succeeded. . . . *Wrote to Mme de Staël*. Dined at Charlotte's. 1. for the second time. This time no doubt whatever . . .

21st. *Letter from Mme de Staël:* She is plaguing me about returning and won't even allow me time to finish my jobs.

25th. Today I enter my fortieth year. *Fugaces labuntur anni* . . .

26th. Day of madness. Delirium of love. What the devil does it mean? It is ten years since I have felt anything like this . . . I want Charlotte, I want her at all costs . . .

But the 'delirium' could only last three days longer, for he had to return to Rouen on the 29th. In this mood of desperation, reawakened passion, consciousness of advancing years, and time flying, he wrote in the diary on the 30th:

Letter from Charlotte. Nowhere else could I find such deep and sweet affection. How many years of happiness lost, even if I recover what I have so foolishly thrown away! *Wrote to Charlotte.* Began a novel which will be our story. Any other work would be out of the question. Boring evening. Scenes. The fault is mine; I must do as little harm as possible. Alas! I am all too clearly doomed to do so some day.

3

But this 'novel' was not *Adolphe*. How could a novel 'which will be our story' possibly be *Adolphe*? But early editions of the diary, and even Jean Mistler in 1945 (quoted by Harold Nicolson in his book in 1949), give this vital entry not only for a different date but as 'a novel which will be *my own story*'. The proper text was not published until 1952, by Alfred Roulin, and it is the one given in the Pléiade edition of Constant's works. Hence all the confusion. Generations of commentators and critics have assumed that this quotation was all that needed to be said about the genesis of *Adolphe*.

But there is a little more. Benjamin worked on for some days with his mind full of Charlotte, but then, on the 10th of November, comes this entry:

... Got on with my episode of Ellenore. I greatly doubt whether I have enough perseverance to finish the novel ...

The 'novel' is already distinct from the 'episode', and already Benjamin is thinking of dealing with the episode separately. Two days later, on the 12th:

... Read my episode in the evening. I think it is very touching, but I shall have a job to go on with the novel.

And on the 14th:

... My episode is nearly finished. My eyes are going wrong with writing at night ...

After an interruption of some days spent in travelling he writes on the 1st of December:

Worked a little at my novel, which bores me.

And on the 21st:

Worked at my novel. When I have done the two chapters which join on to the story and death of Ellenore I shall leave it at that.

The last mention of the novel is on 31st of December, after which the full-scale novel, of which the Ellenore episode was to be a part, seems to have been abandoned. References many years later to reading his novel aloud clearly mean *Adolphe* (the episode) more or less as we know it today.

4

The scholars mentioned earlier busied themselves for years (working on corrupt texts of the *Journal* and, until ten years ago, in ignorance of *Cécile*), pointing out the known facts about Benjamin Constant's life and the departures therefrom in *Adolphe*. They begin at page one and triumphantly indicate that the real Benjamin was sixteen, and not twenty-two, when he left Erlangen, and not Göttingen, and so forth, forgetting the simple and snobbish conventions of a work of fiction whereby, for instance, an Englishman might begin a novel by 'I came down from Oxford' rather than 'I left Redbrick in a hurry after six months'. But art and life are different things, and the game of factual verification leads to a dead end. It is not until the novel is considered on its own merits, until it is realized that its value as a work of art and truth results from the alterations to the mere facts, from a process of simplifying, selecting, and concentrating, that the work is seen to be a masterpiece.

What are Ellenore and Adolphe? Of course the factual framework is the story of Anna Lindsay, the beautiful, ageing, foreign mistress of an aristocrat, and so is Ellenore's submissiveness and limited intelligence. On the other hand the possessiveness, the violence, the scenes, the sending out of a search party to bring back the wandering lover, all these things are from the miserable existence of Benjamin with Mme de Staël. The magic of first love may well be an evocation of happy days with Charlotte, and so one might go on. All that matters is that Ellenore is an amalgam of Benjamin's experience of woman, and that Adolphe, in his relationship with her, feels and behaves as do a large number of normal men. But whereas the ordinary man's experience of what in modern jargon is called the sex-war is diluted by the preoccupations of business and family life, in Ellenore and Adolphe the essential psychological truth is isolated and intensified, as in a tragedy of Racine, by removal of all irrelevant circumstances and manipulation of essential ones in order to throw the main subject into the highest possible relief. In Ellenore the instinct of every woman to seek security, stability, normality, permanency, is intensified by her unsettled childhood and ambiguous, insecure social position. In Adolphe every man's basic vanity, promiscuity, desire for independence, and resentment of trammels is heightened in a motherless son of a cold and distant father, whose longing for affection has never been satisfied, but who is terrified of becoming involved, and that is why he seeks out the easy and flattering conquest of an older woman socially isolated because of her irregular sexual life.

The tragedy of sexual love is that the man by his very nature pursues, wins, and immediately tires, whereas the woman, more slowly aroused, only yields when she has made up her mind. He, once his vanity and desires are satisfied, wants to pass on; she has chosen her mate for life. She tries to hold him by ties of gratitude, seeking to bind him by kindnesses, sacrifices, and forgiveness, and the more she devotes herself the more tired he is of cloying affection, the more he hates being beholden, the more ashamed he is of his own ingratitude, the more he resents being so obviously put in the wrong. Of course in most human beings these tendencies are soon submerged by marriage, children, habit, and advancing years. Were it not so, if these stabilizing influences did not exist, the end would be tragic. In *Adolphe* this tragic end is the only way of getting out of a psychological *impasse*; it is not put there simply because convention, since the days of *Manon Lescaut*, had demanded that heroines of novels should die in an odour of pathos, if not of sanctity.

No work of art is without a point of view, and of course that of *Adolphe* is masculine. That is why the hero is more lucid in his knowledge of himself than in his picture of woman. Lazy, a moral coward, but a master of self-analysis and casuistry, Adolphe uses his intelligence to get what he wants and to avoid or postpone the unpleasant consequences, using ingenious arguments to browbeat self-accusation into acquiescence, to dress up self-interest as prudence or common sense, to transform qualms of conscience into unworthy thoughts over which reason and far-sightedness triumph. He battles with his conscience, but he always wins the battle. He always has an excuse ready, even for reading, immediately after her death, a document he had sworn to Ellenore he would burn unread. Adolphe's debates with himself and self-righteous speeches to Ellenore are miracles of self-betrayal. His character is the great achievement of the book, whereas Ellenore, being a composite figure, may be thought, however true she may be to agreed generalizations about women, to lack the consistency and unity of a supreme artistic creation. But that is for the reader to judge for himself.

5

The details of Benjamin Constant's life after 1807 need not concern us very much. The personal complications and political activities continued, but there was a final break with Mme de Staël in 1811 (when she had fallen passionately in love with John Rocca, a handsome cavalryman over twenty years her junior, who fathered her last child, a boy born in the spring of that year, and who was to be her second husband) a certain weariness with poor Charlotte, now his wife and not as young as she had been, a hopeless passion, in his late forties, for Mme Récamier, whom he had known for many years but not thought of in that way before. Politically very involved during 1814 and the Hundred Days, when he unwisely changed sides and backed the wrong horse, after Waterloo, Benjamin hastened to change back again and wrote an apologia explaining why he was now reconverted to the Bourbon cause. Louis XVIII, a tolerant man, obligingly removed Benjamin's name from the list of Bonapartist proscriptions, but his political future looked very bleak and he decided to go on his travels again, reaching London with Charlotte in January 1816. He stayed in London for many months, moving in society and giving readings of *Adolphe*, which he had at last decided to publish.

The first edition appeared almost simultaneously in London and Paris in mid-June 1816. There were a few typographical differences, such as the order of the names of the publishers on the title page, but they were virtually identical.

Immediately Benjamin was embarrassed by gossip identifying various characters in the novel, and he wrote the following disclaimer to the editor of the *Morning Chronicle*:

Sir,

Various papers have given the public to understand that the short novel of *Adolphe* contains circumstances personal to me and to individuals really existing. I think it my duty to disclaim any such unwarrantable interpretation. I should have thought it foolish in me to describe myself, and surely the very judgement I passed upon the hero of that anecdote ought to have screened me from that suspicion; for no one can take pleasure in representing himself as guilty of vanity, weakness and ingratitude. But the accusation of having described any other person is much more serious. It would fix on my character a stain I can never submit to. Neither Ellenore, nor Adolphe's father, nor the Count of P— have any resemblance to any person I have ever known. Not only my friends, but my acquaintances are sacred to me.

I am, sir, sincerely, your humble obedient servant,

B. de Constant

23 June 1816

Seriously perturbed by the persistent talk, towards the end

of June he wrote a preface, destined to refute such allegations, which he would have ready for a second edition. The very existence of this second French edition was conjectural for many years, and now only four copies are known, none of which I have been able to see.

But while this was going on, an English translation was being prepared under the author's personal supervision by Alexander Walker, his friend and formerly a lecturer at the University of Edinburgh. It was finished by early July and published in London at the end of August. Walker translated the new preface, which was put at the head of the English edition together with this note of recommendation from the author:

In more than one respect, this little novel has met with unusual good fortune; for, besides the flattering approbation the original has obtained, it has also found in my friend, Mr Alexander Walker, late lecturer at Edinburgh, a translator far above the common rank of translators, and well able to gratify the public with original works, but who has condescended to apply to this small volume his profound and refined knowledge of both languages, and has thus rendered the English *Adolphe* completely equal to the French one.

It is Walker's version of this interesting preface which appears at the head of the present translation, all the rest of which I have translated from the best and latest edition, that in the Bibliothèque de la Pléiade, Paris, N.R.F., 1957. The short preface to the third edition (1824), which follows it, is the one usually given in modern editions.

The 'publisher's' notes at the beginning and end form part of the novel itself, and are survivals from the seventeenth- and eighteenth-century tradition whereby a novel was thought to be more credible if made to look like authentic letters or memoirs. Hence the original subtitle, often not even printed today: *An anecdote found among the papers of an unknown person.*

*

The Pléiade edition of the text supersedes everything else because much material was not available to earlier editors. But the edition by Gustave Rudler (Manchester University Press, 1919), although needing supplementation, remains a model of what a critical edition should be. Two biographical works in English will be found absorbingly interesting: Harold Nicolson: *Benjamin Constant*, London, Constable, 1949. J. Christopher Herold: *Mistress to an Age. A Life of Madame de Staël*, London, Hamish Hamilton, 1959. The second is one of the most remarkable books of recent years.

To say that I am grateful to my wife for her help is a ludicrous understatement. Collaboration would be nearer the mark.

August 1962   L.W.T.

PREFACE

to the Second French Edition or an essay on the
character and the moral result of the work*

THE success of this little work rendering a second edition
necessary, I avail myself of the circumstance to prefix to it
some reflections on the character and the moral of an anecdote, on which the attention of the public confers a value
which I was far from attaching to it.

I have already protested against the allusions which malig-
nity, aspiring to the merit of penetration, has, by absurd
conjectures, believed it might discover in it. If I had really
given occasion for such interpretations – if there were found,
in my book, a single phrase which might authorize them, I
should consider myself as deserving severe reproach.

But all these pretended approximations are happily too
vague, and too devoid of truth, to have made any impression.
They have not, moreover, had their origin in the better
classes of Society. They were the invention of those men
who, not being admitted into higher circles, observe them
from without, with an awkward curiosity and a wounded
vanity, and seek to find, or to cause scandal, in a sphere
which is above them.

Scandal is so quickly forgot, that I am perhaps wrong in
speaking of it here. But I have experienced from it a painful
surprize, which has rendered it necessary for me to repeat,
that none of the characters traced in Adolphe has a relation
to any of the individuals whom I know – that I have not
wished to portray in it any one, friendly or indifferent; for,

* Alexander Walker's translation, 1816. See Introduction, § 5. Original spelling and punctuation.

even towards these, I deem myself bound by that tacit engagement of respect and of reciprocal discretion, on which society reposes.

Besides, writers more celebrated than I am, have experienced the same fate. It has been pretended that M. de Chateaubriand has described himself in René; and the woman, who in our times, is at once the most intellectual and the best, Madame de Staël, has been suspected, not only of having depicted herself in Delphine and in Corinne, but of having traced severe portraits of some of her acquaintances:– imputations very little deserved; for, assuredly, the genius which created Corinne had no need of the resources of malice; and all social perfidy is incompatible with the character of Madame de Staël – that character so noble, so courageous under persecution, so faithful in friendship, so generous in devotion. The rage to recognize in works of imagination the individuals whom one meets with in the world, is for these works a real plague. It degrades them, gives them a false direction, destroys their interest, annihilates their utility. To seek for allusions in a romance, is to prefer slander to nature, and to substitute mere gossip for observation of the human heart.

I think, I confess, that there may be found in Adolphe an object more useful, and, I may venture to say so, more elevated.

I have not wished merely to prove the danger of those irregular connexions, where we are usually so much the more shackled as we think ourselves more free. Such a demonstration might well have had its utility. It was not, however, my principal idea.

Independently of those established connexions which society tolerates and condemns, there is in the mere habit of borrowing the language of love, and of giving to oneself, or of exciting in others, transient emotions of the heart, a danger which has not hitherto been sufficiently appreciated. We engage in a career of which we are unable to foresee the end: we know neither what we may inspire, nor what we expose ourselves to experience. We give, in sport, blows of which we calculate neither the force, nor the reaction on ourselves; and the wound which seems slight may be incurable.

Even coquettes do an immensity of ill, though men, more vigorous, more distracted from sentiment by imperious occupations, and destined to serve as a centre for what surrounds them, have not, in the same degree as women, the noble and the dangerous faculty of living in another and for another. But how much more cruel becomes this artifice, which at first sight might be deemed only frivolous, when it is exercised on weak beings, having no real life but in the heart, no deep interest but in the affections, without activity to occupy them, without career to command them, confiding by nature, credulous by an excusable vanity, feeling that their sole existence is to give themselves up without reserve to a protector, and led incessantly to confound the need of protection with the need of love!

I speak not of the positive ills which result from intimacies formed and broken, from the subversion of conditions, from the rigour of public judgement, and from the malevolence of that implacable society, which seems to have found pleasure in placing women over an abyss, in order to condemn them, if they fall into it. There is in these considerations only vulgar evils. – I speak of those sufferings of the heart, of that wretched amazement of a mind deceived, of that surprize with which it learns that confidence becomes a fault, and sacrifices crimes even in the eyes of him who has received them. I speak of that dread which seizes her when she sees herself abandoned by him who swore to protect her; of that distrust which succeeds to a confidence so entire, and which, forced to direct itself against the being who was elevated above all others, extends itself therefore to the rest of the world. I speak of that esteem driven back upon itself, and which knows not where it may place itself.

Even to men themselves, it is not an indifferent matter to do this ill. Almost all of them believe themselves more corrupt, more thoughtless than they are. They expect to be able easily to break the intimacy which they carelessly contract. In the distance, the image of grief appears vague and indistinct, like a cloud which they may pass through without difficulty. A system of unfeeling vanity – a fatal gift, which bequeathes to the folly of the generation which arises the corruption of the generation which has grown old – a mockery become common, but which seduces the mind by satirical combinations, as if any combination could change the basis of things – all that they hear, in a word, and all that they say, seems to arm them against the tears which do not yet flow. But when these tears do flow, nature returns into their breasts, in spite of the factitious atmosphere with which they had surrounded themselves. They feel that a being which suffers because it loves, is sacred. They feel that even in their heart, which they believed not to be engaged in the affair, are deeply sunk the roots of the sentiment which they have inspired; and if they wish to overcome that which they habitually call weakness, it is necessary that they descend into this miserable heart, that they crush there whatever is generous, that they tear asunder whatever is faithful, that they immolate whatever is good. They succeed; but it is by smiting with death one portion of their soul; and they arise from this achievement, having deceived confidence, braved sympathy, abused weakness, insulted morality by rendering it the excuse of obduracy, having prophaned every expression and trampled under foot every sentiment. Thus they survive their better nature, perverted by their victory, or ashamed of that victory, if it have not perverted them.

Some have asked me what Adolphe should have done, to experience and to cause less of affliction? His situation and that of Ellenor [*sic*] were without resources; and that is precisely what I have desired. I have shown him tormented, because he loved Ellenor but feebly; he would not have been less tormented, if he had loved her more. He suffered by her, from want of sentiment; with sentiment more ardent, he would have suffered for her. Society, disapproving and disdainful, would have poured all its venom on the love which its recognition had not sanctioned. It is the never having commenced such connexions which is necessary for the happiness of life: when we have once entered on that career, we have no longer but the choice of evils.

PREFACE
to the Third Edition

IT is not without some hesitation that I have agreed to the reprinting of this little work which was published some ten years ago. Had I not been almost sure that a pirated edition was projected in Belgium, and that this edition, like most of those circulated in Germany and sent into France by Belgian pirates, would be padded out with additions and interpolations in which I had no hand, I should never have bothered with this story, which was written with the sole purpose of proving to one or two friends staying in the country that it was possible to infuse a kind of interest into a novel with characters numbering only two and a situation remaining the same throughout.

Once I was embarked on the work I wanted to develop some further ideas which occurred to me and struck me as being not without a certain utility. What I wanted to describe was the pain inflicted upon even the hardest hearted by the suffering they cause to others, and the illusion which makes them think they are more fickle and corrupt than they really are. From a distance the picture of the grief one causes looks vague and indistinct, like a mist easy to walk through, and one is led on by the approbation of a quite artificial society which substitutes rules for principles and conventions for emotions, which hates scandal because it is a nuisance and not because it is immoral, for it gladly welcomes vice when there is no scandal involved. One thinks that ties thoughtlessly formed can be painlessly broken. But when one sees the agony resulting from such broken ties, the pain and bewilderment of a soul deceived, the mistrust that follows such utter confidence and, when forced to turn against the one person who stands apart from the rest of society, extends to society as a whole; when one sees esteem turned back upon itself and not knowing where else to find an object, then indeed one feels that there is something sacred in a heart that suffers because it loves; one discovers how deep are the roots of a passion one thought one inspired but did not share. And if one rises above what is called weakness, it is by dint of destroying every bit of generosity one has, tearing to pieces all fidelity, sacrificing everything noble and good. One recovers from such a victory, applauded by the friendly and indifferent alike, having dealt a death-blow to part of one's soul, set all sympathy at nought, taken advantage of weakness and offended morality by using it as a pretext for harshness; and one outlives one's better nature, ashamed or perverted after such a miserable success.

Such was the picture I sought to draw in *Adolphe*. I do not know whether I have been successful, but what might incline me to believe I had at any rate a certain quality of truth is that almost all my readers whom I have met have referred to themselves as having been in my hero's position. It is true that a kind of gratified vanity showed through the regret they displayed at all the pain they had caused; they enjoyed representing themselves as having been pursued, like Adolphe, by the unrelenting affection they had inspired, and as victims of the measureless love somebody had conceived for them. I think that for the most part they were maligning themselves, and that had their vanity left them alone their consciences might have rested in peace.

However that may be, everything to do with *Adolphe* has become a matter of supreme indifference to me. I set no store by this novel and repeat that my sole object in allowing it to reappear before a public which has probably forgotten it, even if it ever knew it, has been to declare that any edition containing matter different from what is in this present one is nothing to do with me and I am not responsible.

NOTE BY THE PUBLISHER

Many years ago, when I was travelling in Italy, I was held up by the flooding of the Neto in the little Calabrian village of Cerenza, and had to stay at an inn. There was in the same inn a stranger who had been obliged to stay there for the same reason. He was very silent and looked sad. He showed no impatience. Now and again, as he was the only man in the place to whom I could talk, I grumbled to him about the delay in our journey. 'I don't mind,' he said, 'whether I am here or anywhere else.' According to our host, who had talked to a Neapolitan servant who looked after the stranger but did not know his name, he was not travelling out of curiosity, for he never went to see ruins, picturesque places, monuments or people. He read a good deal, but never continuously, he went for walks in the evening, always alone, and often spent whole days sitting motionless with his head in his hands.

Just when the roads were reopened and we could have set off, the stranger fell seriously ill. I felt bound in ordinary human decency to stay on and look after him. There was only the one village doctor at Cerenza and I wanted to send to Cozenze for better qualified help. 'It is not worth it,' said the stranger; 'this man is exactly what I need.' He was right, and probably more right than he thought, for the man cured him. 'I didn't think you were so clever,' he told him almost peevishly as he dismissed him. He then thanked me for my care and set off.

Some months later, at Naples, I received a letter from our host at Cerenza, with a box found on the Strongoli road, the road that the stranger and I had taken, but separately. The innkeeper who had sent it to me felt sure that it belonged to one of us. The box contained a quantity of very old letters either unaddressed or on which the addresses and signatures were illegible, a woman's portrait and a notebook containing the anecdote or story you are about to read. The stranger to whom these things belonged had gone without leaving me any way of writing to him, and I kept them for ten years, not quite knowing what I ought to do with them, until I happened to mention them quite by chance while talking to some people in a German town, one of whom begged me to let him have the manuscript which was in my possession. A week later the manuscript was returned to me with a letter that I have put at the end of this story because it would be meaningless if it were read before the story itself.

This letter persuaded me to publish now by telling me for certain that publication cannot offend or compromise anybody. I have not changed a single word of the original, and even the suppression of proper names is not my doing; they were indicated in the manuscript, as they still are here, by initials only.

ADOLPHE

Chapter One

I WAS twenty-two and had just finished my studies at the University of Göttingen. My father, a minister under the Elector of —, proposed sending me on a tour of the most interesting European countries, after which I was to be appointed to the staff of his department and trained to succeed him eventually. Although I had led a very dissipated life, I had, by dint of hard study, won distinctions beyond those of my fellow-students which had given my father hopes that were probably very exaggerated.

These hopes had made him very indulgent towards my many peccadilloes. He had never let me suffer the consequences of my foolish conduct, but had always honoured my requests for money and sometimes anticipated them.

Unfortunately his treatment of me was noble and generous rather than affectionate. I was very much aware of all his claims to my gratitude and respect, but there had never been any real understanding between us because there was something cynical in his cast of mind which clashed with my temperament. At that time all I wanted was to give myself up to the kind of primitive and impulsive reactions which lift the soul out of the common rut and make it look upon everyday things with disdain. In my father I found, not indeed a censor, but a detached and caustic observer who would begin a conversation with a pitying smile and soon lose patience and cut it short. I cannot recall ever having had one hour's serious talk with him in the first eighteen years of my life. His letters were affectionate and full of sensible and sympathetic advice, but no sooner were we in each other's presence than there came over him a sort of reserve which

I could not account for and which had a chilling effect on me. At that time I did not know what shyness was – that inner suffering which dogs us even into old age, which takes our deepest feelings and rams them back into our hearts, which freezes the words on our lips, distorts everything we try to say, and only lets us express ourselves in general terms and more or less bitter sarcasm, as though we meant to take revenge on our very emotions for the pain we feel through not being able to communicate them. I did not realize that my father was shy even in front of his own son, and that many a time, after a long wait for some sign of affection from me which his own apparent coolness seemed to discourage, he left me with tears in his eyes and complained to others that I did not love him.

The constraint I felt with him had a great influence upon my character. I was as reserved as he was, but more emotional because I was younger, and I cultivated the habit of keeping all my experiences and plans to myself, relying upon myself alone for the carrying out of those plans, and considering the opinions, interest, help and even the very presence of others as an embarrassment and an obstacle. I got into the way of never speaking about what was in my mind and only putting up with conversation as a tiresome necessity, and then I enlivened it with a perpetual flippancy which made it less irksome and helped me to conceal my real thoughts. Hence a certain inability to let myself go which my friends criticize to this day, and a difficulty in talking seriously which I still find hard to overcome. The result of all this was a passionate desire for independence and at the same time complete impatience with ties holding me down and an insurmountable terror of forming new ones. I was only at ease when quite alone, and to this day the effects of this mental attitude are so strong that when I have to choose between two courses of action, even in the most unimportant matters, I am upset by the presence of on-lookers and my instinct is to run away and do my thinking in peace. And yet I was not as profoundly self-centred as such characteristics would seem to suggest: it is true that I was only interested in myself, but even that interest was not strong. Without being aware of it I nursed in the depths of my being a longing for emotional experience, but as this found no satisfaction it alienated me from all the things which one by one aroused my curiosity. This universal apathy of mine had been deepened by the thought of death which had haunted me from my earliest years. I have never understood how men can so lightly cast it out of their minds. When I was seventeen I had witnessed the death of an aged woman whose remarkable and highly original mind had begun to influence my own. Like so many others this woman had begun her career by sallying forth to conquer society, rejoicing in the possession of moral toughness and a power-ful mind. But she did not understand the ways of the world and, again like so many others, through failing to adapt herself to an artificial but necessary code of behaviour, she had lived to see her hopes disappointed and her youth pass joylessly away, until at last old age had overtaken but not subdued her. In a castle near one of our estates she lived on in disillusioned retirement, her only resource being her intellect, with which she analysed everything. For close on a year we had had endless talks together, in which we had considered life in all its aspects and death as the inevitable end of all. After having talked so much with her about death I saw death strike her down before my eyes.

This event had filled me with a sense of the uncertainty of

destiny and a vague pensiveness which never left me. My favourite authors were the poets who dwelt upon the transitoriness of human life. I felt that no objective was worth striving for. It is somewhat strange that this impression has grown weaker in exact proportion to the passing of the years. Perhaps it is that hope has an element of doubt in it, and that when hope is withdrawn a man's career takes on a more austere but less uncertain quality. Or perhaps it is that life seems all the more real as illusions are dispersed, just as a rocky pinnacle stands out more clearly on the horizon when the clouds melt away.

On leaving Göttingen I went to the little town of D—. This town was the seat of a prince who, like most German princes, ruled over his little territory with a gentle hand, protecting the enlightened men who came to live there, granting absolute freedom of opinion to all, but, being obliged by ancient custom to limit his acquaintance to his courtiers, perforce gathered round him only men who for the most part were dull and mediocre. I was welcomed at this court with the curiosity naturally inspired by any stranger who comes and breaks into the restricted circle of monotonous etiquette. For several months nothing struck me as at all worthy of attracting my attention. I was grateful for the kindness shown to me, but at times I was prevented from taking advantage of it by my shyness, and at others I found such pointless activity wearisome and preferred solitude to the insipid amusements I was invited to share in. I had no strong dislike for anybody, but few people aroused my interest, and lack of interest is what people take offence at, for they ascribe it to affectation or spite and do not want to believe that you are simply bored by them. At times I tried to stifle my boredom and took refuge in stony silence, but this silence was taken for haughtiness. At other times, when

I was tired of my own silence, I ventured on a few pleasant-ries, and once my wit began to move it carried me beyond all bounds. I would find myself disclosing in a single day all the silly things I had been observing for a month. The recipients of these sudden and involuntary bursts of confid-ence did not relish them at all, and they were right, for I was merely indulging an urge to talk, and not really con-fiding in them. The woman who had first developed my ideas had inspired in me an insurmountable aversion from all hackneyed phrases and dogmatic formulae. So when I heard stupid people holding forth complacently about estab-lished and incontrovertible principles of morality, behaviour, and religion (which people of that type usually put in the same class), I felt moved to contradict them, not that I would necessarily have held opposite views myself, but because such ponderous, unshakeable convictions exasperated me. In any case some warning instinct made me mistrust general axioms uttered without any reservations, so innocent of any shade of distinction. Fools keep their moral code in a compact and indivisible whole so that it may interfere as little as possible with their actions and leave them their freedom in all matters of detail.

This sort of behaviour soon earned me a name for shallow-ness, sarcastic wit and malice. My bitter words were taken as proofs of a spiteful disposition, my jokes as attacks on all the most respectable things. The people I had unwisely poked fun at found it convenient to identify themselves with the principles they accused me of throwing into doubt. Because I had unwittingly made them laugh at each other's expense they all combined against me. It was just as though by pointing out their funny little ways I had betrayed their confidence, or as if by exhibiting themselves to me as they really were they had extracted from me a promise of silence.

I was not aware of having subscribed to any such agreement, which would have been too binding. They had enjoyed indulging in unbridled self-revelation and I had enjoyed watching them at it and describing what I saw; what they now called a betrayal seemed to me quite a harmless and legitimate compensation for what I had had to put up with.

I am not seeking to make excuses: self-justification is the facile and frivolous resort of the inexperienced, and I have given it up long ago. I simply mean to say (and this is for the benefit of others, not myself, for I am now safe from the attacks of society) that mankind, as it has been moulded by self-interest, affectation, vanity, and fear, takes a great deal of getting used to. A young man's astonishment when he beholds the artificial and highly-wrought thing called society is a sign of a natural heart rather than of a spiteful mind. Not, of course, that society is in any danger; it presses down so heavily upon us and its imperceptible influence is so strong that it soon moulds us into the universal pattern. And then we are no longer surprised, unless it be at our own former surprise, and we feel quite at home in our new character, just as we eventually breathe quite freely in a stuffy, crowded theatre, whereas when we first came in we found the greatest difficulty in breathing at all.

The few who escape this general fate lock their secret disagreement in their hearts: they can see that most ridiculous mannerisms contain incipient vices, and they give up joking about them because contempt has taken the place of amusement, and contempt is silent.

And so vague misgivings about my character began to spread through this limited society. Nobody could point to any reprehensible act of mine, nobody could even deny me credit for acts apparently springing from generosity or

.devotion to duty, but it was said that I was an immoral and unreliable person. These two epithets are happy inventions calculated to suggest things we are ignorant of, and leave people to guess what we do not know.

Chapter Two

LISTLESS, unobservant, bored as I was, I never noticed the impression I was making, and I divided my time between studies which were frequently interrupted, plans I failed to carry out, and amusements which scarcely interested me at all. And then an apparently quite trivial event led to a radical change in my outlook.

For some time a young man with whom I was fairly intimate had been paying attention to one of the less vapid women in our circle, and he had chosen me as a disinterested party in whom to confide his aspirations. After a long campaign he succeeded in winning her love, and as he had not hidden his sorrows and rebuffs from me he felt obliged to tell me about his triumphs. His demonstrations of joy knew no bounds. The sight of such happiness made me regret not having tried such an experience myself, for until then I had had no affair with a woman which could possibly have flattered my self-esteem, and a new future seemed to unfold before my eyes and a fresh need stir into life in my heart. Of course there was a great deal of vanity in it, but it was not merely vanity, and perhaps there was less of it than I believed myself. Man's emotions are so confused and tangled, they are made up of countless impressions unrecognized by the observer, and language, always too crude and generalized, can point them out but never really define them.

In my father's home I had adopted a somewhat immoral attitude towards women. My father was a strict observer of outward appearances, but he quite often indulged in loose talk about love-affairs. He looked upon them, if not as legitimate amusements, at any rate as excusable ones, and in his view marriage alone was a serious matter. His principle was that a young man must carefully avoid committing what is called a 'folly', that is to say embarking on a permanent relationship with anybody not fully his equal in wealth, birth and the obvious social advantages. But apart from that, so long as marriage was not contemplated, there was no harm in taking any woman and then dropping her. I had seen him smile, almost with approval, at this parody of the well-known saying: *It does them so little harm and gives us so much pleasure!*

It is not sufficiently realized what a deep impression sayings of this kind make upon the very young and the extent to which, at an age when all their opinions are still unformed and fluid, children are amazed to see strict rules that have been laid down for them contradicted by jokes enjoyed by all. Such rules cease to be for them anything more than empty phrases which their parents see fit to repeat in order to satisfy their own consciences, whereas the jokes seem to contain the true secret of life.

In my state of vague emotional torment I decided that I wanted to be loved, and looked about me. But I saw nobody who inspired love in me or looked likely to feel any. I studied my own heart and tastes and could not discover any definite preferences. While I was in the throes of this internal debate I made the acquaintance of Count P—, a man of forty whose family was connected with mine. He invited me to go and see him. Ill-fated visit! Living in his house was his mistress, a Polish woman noted for her beauty, though she was past her first youth. In spite of her anomalous position this woman had more than once proved the superiority of her character. She came of an illustrious family which had been ruined during the troubles in Poland; her father had been banished and her mother had sought refuge in France, taking her daughter with her, and there, after her death, she had left her alone in the world. Count P— had fallen in love with her. I have never known how this liaison came about, but when I first saw Ellenore it was long established and so to speak hallowed by time. Was it that her plight was inevitable or was it the inexperience of youth that had thrown her into a way of life repugnant alike to her upbringing, habits and the pride that was one of the most remarkable traits of her character? What I do know and what everybody knew is that when Count P—'s fortune had been reduced to next to nothing and his personal freedom jeopardized, Ellenore had given him such proofs of her loyalty, had repulsed the most brilliant offers with such scorn, had shared his poverty and dangers with so much zeal and even joy, that the most fastidiously censorious could not help doing justice to the purity of her motives and unselfishness of her behaviour. It was thanks to her energy, courage and good sense, and the sacrifices of all kinds that she had borne uncomplainingly that her lover had been able to recover part of his property. They had come to D— to attend to a lawsuit which might restore the whole of the Count's former wealth, and expected to stay there about two years.

Ellenore was no more than ordinarily intelligent, but her ideas were sound, and her speech, though always simple, was sometimes striking because of the high-minded nobility of the sentiments she expressed. She had many prejudices, but they were all directly opposed to her own interests. Because of the very irregularity of her own life according to generally accepted tenets, she set great store by correctness of behaviour. She was deeply religious because religion sternly condemned her way of life. In conversation she strongly discouraged what to other women might have seemed harmless jokes, because she was always afraid that owing to her position people might think themselves free to make un-called-for remarks to her. She would have preferred to receive in her house none but men of the highest rank and most irreproachable lives because those women with whom she shuddered to be compared usually surround themselves with mixed company and merely choose amusing friends, having resigned themselves to the loss of public respect. In a word, Ellenore was continually fighting against her destiny. Every one of her words and deeds was, so to speak, a protest against the class to which she found herself relegated, and as she felt that the facts of the case were stronger than she was and that whatever she tried to do could not alter the position in any way, she was very unhappy. The two children she had had by the Count were being brought up very strictly, and at times you might have said that in the passionate rather than loving care she lavished on them she was expressing a secret revolt, and that they were almost unwanted. When anybody made some well-intentioned remark to her about how the children were growing, how clever they promised to be, or what sort of career they ought to take up, she visibly paled at the thought that some day she would have to tell them about their birth. But if there were the slightest danger, or if she were away for a single hour, she came back to them with an anxiety in which you could see a kind of remorse and a desire to give them happiness by caresses in which she found no pleasure herself. This contrast between her real sentiments and the place she occupied in society had made her emotionally unstable. Often she would be pensive and silent, but at times she would pour forth torrents of words. As she was haunted by one particular obsession, she was never quite self-possessed even during the most general conversation. But for that very reason there was something impetuous and unexpected in her manner that made her more attractive than she would have been by nature. In her, strangeness of situation made up for lack of new ideas. People watched her with the mingled curiosity and interest inspired by a magnificent tempest.

Coming into my consciousness just when my heart was longing for affection and my vanity needed success, Ellenore seemed a conquest worthy of me. For her part she found enjoyment in the company of a man different from any she had so far met. Her circle consisted of a few friends or relations of her lover and their wives, who had been forced by the Count's prestige to acknowledge his mistress. The husbands were no more provided with feelings than with ideas, and the wives only differed from their husbands because there was something more restless and active about their dullness, since they lacked that placidity of mind which derives from having regular occupation and business to attend to. My lighter, more amusing, and varied conversation, my peculiar blend of melancholy and gaiety, apathy and interest, enthusiasm and mockery, came as a surprise to Ellenore and appealed to her. She spoke several languages, imperfectly I admit, but always fluently and sometimes with elegance. Her ideas seemed to emerge all the more pleasing, fresh, and novel because they had to fight their way through such obstacles, for foreign tongues, by removing stock expressions which make our ideas seem either commonplace or affected, give them new life. We read English poets together and went for walks. I often called on her in the morning and again in the evening, and I discussed all sorts of things with her.

I thought I was a cool impartial observer exploring her mind and character, but every word she uttered seemed to me clothed in ineffable grace. My desire to please her gave me a new interest in life and enlivened my existence in a quite unaccustomed way. I attributed this almost magical effect to her charm, and I would have enjoyed it even more fully had I not given certain hostages to my own vanity. This vanity stood as a third party between Ellenore and me. I considered myself in honour bound to make as quickly as possible for the goal I had set myself, and because of this I was not wholeheartedly giving myself up to my impressions. I was impatient to declare myself, for it seemed to me that I had only to speak in order to succeed. I did not think I was in love with Ellenore, but already I could not endure the thought of not pleasing her. She was continually in my thoughts: I made countless plans and invented countless ways of winning her, with that callow fatuity which is so confident of success because it has never attempted anything.

And yet I was checked by an invincible shyness. All my fine speeches died on my lips or ended up quite differently from what I had intended. Within me a battle was raging and I was furious with myself.

Accordingly I looked round for some rationalization which would enable me to emerge from this struggle with my self-esteem intact. I persuaded myself that nothing should be rushed, that Ellenore was all too unprepared for the declaration I contemplated making, and that it would be wiser to wait a little longer. Nearly always, so as to live at peace with ourselves, we disguise our own impotence and weakness as calculation and policy; it is our way of placating that half of our being which is in a sense a spectator of the other.

This state of affairs dragged on. Each day I settled on the morrow as the final date for an unequivocal declaration, and each morrow went by like the day before. As soon as I left Ellenore my diffidence vanished and at once I took up my clever plans and subtle schemes again, but scarcely was I back by her side before I found myself nervous and trembling once more. Anyone who could have read my heart while I was away from her would have taken me for a cold and heartless seducer, but if he could have seen me with her he would have recognized in me the inexperienced, tongue-tied and passionate lover. Either conclusion would have been equally wrong, for there is never any real consistency in mankind, and hardly anybody is wholly sincere or wholly deceitful.

Convinced by these repeated experiences that I should never find the courage to speak to Ellenore, I made up my mind to write. The Count was away. My long drawn out battle against my own character, the irritation I felt at not having been able to overcome it, and my doubts about my chances of success all combined to tinge my letter with an emotional colour scarcely distinguishable from love. And indeed, warmed up as I was by my own rhetoric, by the time I had finished writing I really felt some of the passion I had been at such pains to express.

Ellenore read into my letter what it was natural to read, the passing infatuation of a youngster ten years her junior whose heart was opening to hitherto unknown emotions and who was more deserving of compassion than of anger. Her answer was kind, full of affectionate advice, and offered her true friendship, but she made it clear that she could not see me again before the Count's return.

I was stunned. Inflamed by this setback, my imagination took possession of my whole life. Suddenly I found myself racked by the torments of love which but an hour before I had been simulating with such self-congratulation. I rushed to Ellenore's house only to be told that she was out. I wrote again imploring her to see me for the last time, describing my despair in heartrending terms, and the sinister projects her cruel verdict had put into my mind. For the greater part of that day I vainly waited for an answer, and I could only calm my unspeakable suffering by repeatedly promising myself that next day I would brave every difficulty, seek her out, and speak to her. That evening I received a few words from her, and they were kind. I thought I could detect a hint of sadness and regret, but she stood by her resolve and said it was unshakeable. Next day I again presented myself at her house. She had left for a place in the country and the servants did not know the address. They could not even send on letters.

For a long time I stood there motionless at her door, unable to think of any further possibility of finding her. I was amazed by the intensity of my own suffering, recollecting the times when I had told myself that I was only out for a conquest, that this was just a campaign which I could call off without any trouble. I had no conception then of the violent pain which was implacably tearing my heart asunder. Several days went by in this way. I could neither study nor find distraction in amusement, but ceaselessly walked to and fro past her door. I wandered about the town as though in the hope of meeting her round each corner. One morning, while I was aimlessly walking about in this way, trying to drive away my distress by fatigue, I saw Count P—'s carriage bringing him back from his travels. He recognized me and got out. After a few commonplaces I mentioned Ellenore's sudden departure, trying to hide my anxiety. 'Oh, yes,' he said, 'one of her friends who lives a few miles away has had some trouble or other, and Ellenore thought her comforting presence would be a help. She went off without consulting me. She is the slave of her emotions, and her heart is always so restless that she finds something akin to peace in devotion to others. But I need her here too badly, and I shall write to her. She will certainly be back in a few days' time.'

This reassured me and my distress grew perceptibly less.

For the first time since Ellenore's departure I could breathe freely. She did not come back as soon as the Count had hoped, but I had taken up my normal routine again and the anguish I had suffered was beginning to fade away when a month later M. de P— sent a message saying that Ellenore was due back that evening. As he attached great importance to maintaining her in a social position in keeping with her character but from which her situation seemed to preclude her, he had invited to supper several women relations and friends who had consented to see her.

My memories came back, jumbled at first, but soon much more precise. My pride was involved and I was embarrassed and humiliated by the prospect of seeing once again the woman who had treated me like a baby. I visualized her smiling as I came up to her at the way in which a short absence had calmed a young hothead's effervescence, and I read into that smile a kind of scorn. Gradually my passion revived. That morning I had got up quite free from thoughts of Ellenore, but an hour after hearing that she was coming back the vision of her was floating before my eyes, holding sway over my heart. I was terrified of not seeing her.

I stayed indoors all day, as it were in hiding, for I was in terror lest the slightest movement on my part might prevent our meeting. And yet nothing could be more certain and straightforward, but I was looking forward to it so intensely that it seemed as if it could not happen. I was tortured with impatience and looked at my watch every minute. My pulse beat so feverishly in my veins that I had to open the window for air.

At last I heard the hour strike for me to set off for the Count's. And at once my impatience turned into apprehension; I took my time over dressing and no longer felt any hurry to get there. I was so afraid that my expectations would be disappointed and so acutely conscious of the grief I ran the risk of feeling that I would gladly have agreed to postpone the whole thing.

It was getting late when I reached M. de P—'s house. I saw Ellenore sitting at the far end of the room but dared not go up to her, feeling that all eyes were fixed upon me. I went and hid in a corner behind a group of men who were chatting, and from there I watched her. She seemed slightly changed, a little paler than usual. The Count saw me in the sort of retreat to which I had withdrawn, and he came over to me, took my hand and led me to Ellenore. 'May I introduce,' he said laughingly, 'one of the men who was most shocked by your unexpected departure.' Ellenore was talking to a lady sitting by her, and when she saw me the words died on her lips and she was quite at a loss. I felt not a little awkward myself.

As we could easily be overheard I asked her some quite general questions, and we both recovered some semblance of calm. Supper was announced and I offered her my arm, which she could not refuse to take. 'Unless you promise to see me here tomorrow at eleven,' I said as we went along, 'I shall leave at once, abandon country, family, and father, break off all my connexions, abjure all my obligations and go away, anywhere, and seek the speediest end to a life you are plaguing for your amusement.' 'Adolphe!' she answered, and then paused. I made as if to go. I do not know what sort of expression I had on my face, but I had never before felt such a violent spasm of pain. Ellenore looked at me with mingled terror and affection. 'I will see you tomorrow,' she said, 'but I do beg of you ...' She could not finish the sentence as there were many people following us. I pressed her hand with my arm. We took our places at table.

I should have liked to sit next to Ellenore, but the master

of the house had settled it otherwise, and I was put almost opposite her. At the beginning of the meal she was pre-occupied. If spoken to she answered pleasantly enough, but soon lapsed into dreaminess. One of her friends was so struck by her silence and depression that she asked her if she was feeling well. 'No, I have not been feeling very well just lately,' she replied, 'and even now I feel anything but my real self.' I wanted to make a good impression upon Ellenore and, by showing how charming and witty I was, win her admiration and prepare her for the interview she had agreed to give me. So I tried countless ways of holding her attention. I led the conversation round to topics I knew interested her, and our table companions joined in. Her presence inspired me and I managed to catch her ear and soon saw her smile. This so filled my heart with joy and my eyes showed such gratitude that she could not help being touched. Her gloomy preoccupation melted away and she gave up fighting against the secret spell cast over her soul by the sight of the happi-ness she was giving me. When we rose from table our hearts were in complete harmony as though we had never been parted. 'You see,' I said as I gave her my hand to lead her back to the drawing-room, 'my whole life is in your hands. What have I done that you should take pleasure in making that life a torment?'

Chapter Three

I SPENT a sleepless night. The stage of calculations and intrigues was over and I felt in my heart of hearts that I was really in love. It was no longer the prospect of a triumph that spurred me on; I was possessed to the exclusion of all else by the need to see the woman I loved and enjoy being with her. It struck eleven and I went to Ellenore; she was waiting for me. She wanted to speak, but I asked her to listen to me. I sat down beside her, for I could scarcely find the strength to stand up, and I went on in these terms, though not without frequent pauses:

'I have not come to appeal against the sentence you have passed, nor do I propose to withdraw a declaration which may have offended you, for I could not even if I wanted to. The love you are rejecting cannot be destroyed; the very effort I am making at this moment to speak to you with some semblance of calm is a proof of the strength of an emotion which distresses you. But the time for talking about that has gone by, and this is not the reason why I have begged you to give me a hearing. On the contrary I have come to ask you to put it out of your mind and let me come and see you as in the past. Set aside the thought of a moment's madness, and do not punish me because you know a secret I ought to have locked in my heart. You know all about me and this character of mine which people call difficult and uncouth, this heart of mine which is indifferent to all wordly interests, solitary even amidst crowds of men, and yet resentful of the solitude to which it is condemned. My one support has been your friendship, and without it I cannot live. I have got into the habit of seeing you, and you have allowed this pleasant

55

habit to take root and grow. What have I done to deserve losing the one consolation of such a dull and tedious existence? I am miserably unhappy and feel I have not the strength left to endure such prolonged wretchedness. I have no hopes, no requests to make except to see you, but see you I must if I am to go on living.'

Ellenore remained silent. 'What are you afraid of?' I went on. 'What demands am I making? Only what you freely give to all and sundry. Are you afraid of society? But society will be too absorbed in its own solemn round of frivolities to want to peer into a heart like mine. Why should I be anything but prudent? Does not my life depend upon it? Ellenore, listen to this entreaty of mine; you will not go unrewarded. You will feel the charm of being loved in this way, of seeing me near you, concerned with your welfare alone, living only for you, and finding in you any sensation of happiness I am still capable of feeling if once your presence saves me from misery and despair.'

I went on in this way for some time, brushing aside all obstacles and continually turning to my advantage any arguments which might work in my favour. I was so meek and submissive, I was asking for so little, and a refusal would have made me so unhappy!

All this affected Ellenore. She laid down several conditions, agreed to see me, but only occasionally and when many others were present, stipulated that I should never talk of love. I promised whatever she wanted. Each of us was well pleased, for I was happy to have regained the ground I had been in danger of losing, and she to find herself being generous and responsive yet at the same time prudent.

The very next day I took advantage of the permission I had been given, and on the following days I behaved in the same way. Ellenore soon ceased to think about the necessity of my visits being infrequent, and soon nothing seemed more natural than that she should see me every day. Ten years of loyalty on her part had made M. de P— completely trustful and he left Ellenore the greatest freedom. As he had had to fight against public opinion which had tried to exclude his mistress from the society in which he was called upon to live so now he was glad to see Ellenore's circle widening, for in his view a houseful of guests was the best proof of his victory over people's prejudices.

Whenever I arrived I could see an expression of pleasure in Ellenore's eyes. If a conversation was to her liking she instinctively looked in my direction, and nothing of interest was said without her calling me in to listen. But she was never alone, and whole evenings passed by without my ever being able to have any private word with her beyond a few snatches of trivial or interrupted talk. So much restraint very soon irritated me and I grew morose, taciturn, moody, and sarcastic. If anyone else spoke to Ellenore alone I had the utmost difficulty in controlling my resentment, and I often rudely broke in. Little did I care whether I gave offence, neither was I always held back by fear of compromising her. She reproached me for my change of attitude. 'What do you expect?' I said angrily. 'I suppose you think you have done a great deal for me, but I am obliged to tell you that you are mistaken. I cannot understand your new way of living at all. You used to live very quietly, you had a horror of tiring social gatherings and avoided those interminable conversations which go on and on for the very reason that they ought never to have been started. But now you keep open house to the whole world. It is as though by asking you to let me come and see you I have obtained permission for the whole universe to share the same favour. I confess that when I used to see how circumspect you were I never expected you would become so frivolous.'

The look of resentment and sadness I thought I could read in Ellenore's face made me suddenly soften my tone. 'Dearest Ellenore,' I pleaded, 'do I not deserve to be distinguished from the hordes of tiresome people who beset you? Has not friendship its own secrets? Is it not natural for a friend to lose heart and take umbrage amidst the din of the mob?'

Ellenore was afraid that if she showed herself inflexible it might lead to a resumption of the rash behaviour which alarmed her both for herself and for me. The thought of breaking with me did not enter her mind, and she consented to see me sometimes alone.

From that moment the strict rules she had laid down became rapidly slacker. She let me talk of my love and soon grew accustomed to such language. Before long she confessed that she loved me.

I spent some hours at her feet, calling myself the happiest of men and lavishing upon her countless assurances of my love, devotion and undying respect. She told me all she had suffered while trying to tear herself away from me, how many times she had hoped I would guess her secret despite her efforts to keep it hidden, how every little sound she heard seemed to herald my arrival, her embarrassment, fear, and joy when she did see me, and how her self-distrust had made her throw herself into social amusements in order to reconcile prudence with the promptings of her heart by cultivating the crowds of people she had formerly avoided. I made her tell me the most trifling details over and over again, and an episode that had lasted only a few weeks seemed to us like a life-story, for love has a sort of magic which makes up for long-standing memories. All other human affections need a history, but love, like an enchantment, can create a past to surround us with. It gives us, so to speak, the feeling of having lived for years with a person who until recently was almost a stranger. Love is only a single speck of light, yet it seems to illumine the whole of time. A few days ago it did not exist, and soon it will have ceased to be, but so long as it does exist it sheds its radiance upon the time which has preceded it as upon that which is to come.

But this calm was short lived. The haunting memory of her previous frailties had put Ellenore all the more on her guard against her own weakness, whilst my imagination and desires, together with a concept of the art of love, the fatuity of which I hardly noticed myself, all rebelled against this kind of love. Always cowardly, often exasperated, I grumbled, stormed, heaped reproaches upon her. More than once she thought of breaking a tie which was bringing nothing but worry and torment into her life, but each time I placated her with entreaties, disclaimers and tears.

One day I wrote to her in these terms:

'Ellenore, you do not realize all I am going through. With you or away from you I am equally miserable. During the hours of separation from you I wander to and fro, weighed down by the burden of an intolerable existence. Company I find irksome, but solitude drives me mad. All these people who stare at me with an indifferent eye, who, knowing nothing of what is going on in my mind, look on with dull curiosity and callous astonishment, yet dare to talk to me about some other topic than you, fill my heart with mortal pain. I keep out of their way, but when I am alone I try in vain to find some fresh air to fill my choking lungs. I fling myself down upon the earth that ought to open and swallow me for ever. I rest my head on a cold stone that ought to cool the burning fever which consumes me. I drag myself up that hill from which your house can be seen and there I stay with my eyes fixed on the home I shall never share with you. If only I had met you sooner you might have belonged to me! I might have held in my arms the only being formed by nature for my heart – this heart which has endured so much in its search for you and now has found you too late! When these times of insane despair have at last gone by and the moment comes for seeing you again I set out for your house trembling and afraid that all the passers-by are guessing my innermost feelings. I stop, walk slowly, put off the moment of bliss, bliss which is constantly being threatened and which I always think I am on the point of losing. For it is an imperfect and chequered happiness, and probably at every minute of the day something is working against it: either malignant events, the eyes of jealous onlookers, purely arbitrary caprices of fate or your own will! When I reach your door and open it I am seized by a fresh panic and steal forward like a criminal, begging mercy of everything I meet as though each inanimate object were hostile and begrudged me the moment of felicity that is still to be enjoyed. I am scared by the least sound, and the slightest movement terrifies me; the very sound of my own footsteps makes me recoil. Even when I am within reach of you I still dread some obstacle which might suddenly thrust itself between you and me. At last I see you, see you and breathe again, I contemplate you, I stand like a fugitive who has set foot in some place of sanctuary which will protect him from death. But even then, when my whole being leaps towards you, when I sorely need rest after so many tribulations, need to lay my head in your lap and let my tears flow freely, I have to control myself sternly – even with you I have to live a life of strain with never a moment of abandon when I can let my feelings go! Your eyes are examining me, and you are puzzled and almost offended by my emotion. Some unaccountable reserve has taken the place of those wonderful hours when you did at least own that you loved me. Time flies and new interests absorb you; now you never have them out of your mind and you never postpone the time for me to go. Strangers appear, and so I may no longer look at you. I feel obliged to leave in order to turn away the suspicion that surrounds me. And so I go away more upset, more agonized and frenzied than before. I leave you and relapse into that awful loneliness in which I twist and turn and never find a single soul on whom I can rely or who can give me a moment's respite.'

Ellenore had never been loved in this way. M. de P— was genuinely fond of her, most grateful for her devotion to him and full of respect for her character, but in his manner there had always been a hint of superiority towards a woman who had openly given herself to him without his having married her. The general opinion was that he might have contracted a more honourable connexion. He never said such a thing to her and possibly never even to himself, but what is unsaid exists none the less, and whatever exists can be guessed. Until now Ellenore had had no conception of passionate emotion, another's life merged completely in hers, which my very frenzy, my unfairness and reproaches went to prove all the more conclusively. Her resistance had intensified all my sensations and ideas, and now I returned to terrifying bursts of rage, submissiveness, tenderness and idolatrous veneration. I looked upon her as a sacred being and my love was closely allied to religion. And that appealed to her all the more strongly because she was always afraid of being humiliated in the opposite way. In the end she gave herself to me without reserve.

Woe to the man who in the first moments of a love-affair does not believe that it will last for ever! Woe to him who even in the arms of the mistress who has just yielded to him maintains an awareness of trouble to come and foresees that he may later tear himself away! At the moment when she abandons herself to her passion every woman is in a sense touching and sublime. It is not sensual pleasure, not nature, nor our bodies which corrupt us; it is the scheming to which life in society accustoms us and the reflections to which experience gives rise. I loved and respected Ellenore a thousand times more after she had given herself to me. I walked proudly among men and looked upon them with the eye of a conqueror. The very air I breathed was a pure delight. I eagerly went out to meet nature and thank her for the immense and unhoped-for gift she had deigned to bestow on me.

Chapter Four

THE magic of love – who could ever describe it? Certainty of having found the one being destined for us by nature, sudden light shed upon life itself and apparently explaining its mystery, unsuspected value conferred upon the most trifling circumstances, flying hours whose details elude the memory through their very sweetness, leaving nothing but a long trail of bliss in our souls, fun and laughter that sometimes breaks unbidden into our usual tenderness, such pleasure when together and such hope when apart, detachment from all mundane cares and superiority over everything round us, conviction that henceforth the world cannot harm us in our fastness, mutual understanding that divines each thought and responds to every emotion – the magic of love that none who has known can ever describe!

Urgent business obliged M. de P— to be away for six weeks. I spent this time with Ellenore almost without a break. Her attachment to me seemed to have been strengthened by the sacrifice she had made. She never let me leave her without trying to keep me back. When I went out she asked me when I would return. A separation of two hours she found unbearable, and she settled the exact time of my return with anxious precision. I entered into all this with joy, for I was grateful and happy because of the feeling she showed for me. And yet the affairs of ordinary life cannot be forced to fit in with all our desires. It was sometimes awkward to have my every step marked out for me in advance and all my moments counted. I was obliged to hurry through everything I did and break with most of my acquaintances. I did not know what to say to my friends when they invited me to take part in some social activity which in normal circumstances I should have had no reason for declining. When I was with Ellenore I did not hanker after these pleasures of social life which had never appealed to me very strongly, but I would have liked her to leave me freer to give them up of my own accord. It would have been pleasanter to go back to her of my own free will, without telling myself that time was up and she was anxiously waiting, and without the thought of my happiness at rejoining her being mingled with that of her displeasure. Ellenore was a great joy in my life, of course, but she was no longer an objective, she had become a tie. Moreover I was afraid of embarrassing her by my continual presence, which could not fail to surprise her servants and children who might be watching me. I trembled at the thought of upsetting the whole of her life. It seemed to me that we could not be united for ever, and that I was in duty bound to respect her peace; and so I advised prudence while insisting upon my love. But the more advice of this kind I gave her, the less inclined she was to heed what I said. At the same time I was terribly afraid of hurting her, and as soon as I saw an expression of pain on her face my will became the slave of hers, for I was not happy unless she was pleased with me. If, by dint of insisting upon the necessity of my presence elsewhere for a short time, I did manage to get away, I was haunted by the vision of the suffering I had brought upon her until a feverish remorse came over me which grew and grew until it was irresistible. Then I would rush back to her, overjoyed at the prospect of consoling and pacifying her. But as I drew nearer to her house there crept into my other feelings one of resentment at the strange sway she held over me. Ellenore on her side was uncontrolled. I believe she felt towards me in a way she had never felt towards anybody else before. In her previous relationships her heart had been chilled by an irk-some feeling of dependence, but with me she was perfectly at ease because we were on a perfectly equal footing; she had recovered her self-respect by a love free from all calculation and self-interest, for she knew that I was sure she loved me for myself alone. But her giving herself to me thus un-reservedly meant that she concealed none of her changes of mood, so that when I came back into her room, resentful at being back earlier than I would have liked, it would be to find her upset or annoyed. For two hours I had been miser-able away from her because I thought she might be miserable away from me, and now I had two hours of misery with her before being able to restore her spirits.

Yet I was not unhappy, for I told myself it was sweet to be loved, even possessively, and I felt I was doing her good. Her happiness was essential to me and I knew I was essential for her happiness.

Moreover a vague notion, and in many ways a saddening one, that in the very nature of things this liaison could not last helped to calm me in my fits of weariness and im-patience. Ellenore's ties with Count P—, our difference in age and standing, my departure that various circumstances had postponed but which was imminent, were so many arguments in favour of my giving and receiving as much happiness as possible. I thought I was sure of the years, and so did not begrudge the days.

Count P— returned. He very soon suspected my relation-ship with Ellenore, and each day his welcome was cooler and more sullen. I spoke strongly to Ellenore about the risks she was running and begged her to let me suspend my visits for a few days, pointing out that the future of her reputation, fortune, and children was at stake. She listened in silence for a long time, pale as death. At length she said:

'Whatever happens you will be going away soon; don't let us anticipate that moment and don't worry about me. Let us save a few days and hours – days and hours are all I need. Some presentiment tells me, Adolphe, that I shall die in your arms.'

And so we went on living as before: I always on edge, Ellenore always sad, and the Count taciturn and pre-occupied. At last the expected letter arrived; my father ordered me home. I took the letter to Ellenore. 'Already!' she said when she had read it, 'I didn't think it would be so soon.' Giving in to her tears she took my hand and said: 'Adolphe, you see I cannot live without you. I don't know what will happen to me in the future, but I do beg of you not to go yet. Find excuses for staying, ask your father to let you prolong your stay for six months. Is six months so very long?' I wanted to break her determination, but she was crying so bitterly and trembling, and her face bore the marks of such heartbreaking suffering, that I could not go on. I fell at her feet, threw my arms round her, swore I loved her, and then went off to write to my father. And indeed I wrote under the impulse that Ellenore's grief had inspired. I alleged a thousand reasons for this delay; I stressed the advisability of going on with some courses of study at D— that I had not been able to take at Göttingen. When I posted the letter I desperately wanted to get the consent I was asking for.

That evening I went back to Ellenore. She was sitting on a sofa, Count P— was some distance away near the fireplace and the children were at the other end of the room, not play-ing, but wearing on their faces that puzzled look of children conscious of some upset the cause of which they cannot fathom. I signalled to Ellenore that I had done what she wanted. Her eyes lit up with joy but soon clouded over again. Not a word was spoken. The silence grew embarrassing for all three. 'I am told, Sir,' the Count said at last, 'that you are ready to leave.' I answered that I was not aware of it. 'At your age,' he went on, 'it seems to me that one ought not to delay beginning on a career. But of course,' he added, looking at Ellenore, 'everybody here may not think as I do.'

My father's reply came with all speed. As I opened the letter I trembled at the thought of the grief a refusal would inflict upon Ellenore. I even felt that I would be as grief-stricken as she was; but as I read the consent he agreed to give, all the disadvantages of an extension to my stay suddenly leapt to my mind. 'Six more months of embarrassment and constraint!' I exclaimed to myself; 'six months during which I shall be sinning against a man who has befriended me, exposing to danger a woman who loves me. I am running the risk of depriving her of the only situation in which she might be able to live in peace and with the respect of all. I am deceiving my father, and what for? So as not to have to face for one moment the prospect of a painful scene which is inevitable sooner or later. But aren't we going through this pain every day, by slow degrees and drop by drop? I am doing nothing but harm to Ellenore, and my feeling for her, whatever it is, cannot satisfy her. I am sacrificing myself for her without any effect upon her happiness, and I myself am existing uselessly, with no independence, not a moment's freedom, no chance of breathing in peace for a single hour.' I was full of these reflections as I went in to Ellenore. She was alone. 'I am staying six months longer,' I said. 'Your announcement sounds very bald.' 'Well, I admit I am very nervous about the consequences of this extension for both of us.' 'It seems to me that they can't be so very unfortunate for you, at any rate.' 'You know perfectly well, Ellenore, that it is never for myself that I am most concerned.' 'It is hardly for other people's happiness, either.' The conversation had taken a stormy turn. Ellenore was hurt by my regrets in a situation in which she thought I ought to share her joy, whilst I was annoyed at the victory she had won over my earlier resolves. The scene became violent and we burst into mutual recriminations. Ellenore accused me of having deceived her, of having only a passing fancy for her, of having lost her the Count's affection, of having cast her back into the dubious situation she had been trying to get out of all through her life. I was angry to see her using against me the things I had done solely out of obedience to her and fear of upsetting her, and so I complained of the constraint I was being subjected to, of my youth being wasted in inactivity, of the way she was tyrannizing over my every movement. But as I was speaking I saw her face suddenly wet with tears; I stopped, went back on my own words, retracted, explained. We embraced, but a first blow had been struck, a first frontier crossed. We had both said irreparable things; we might be able to stop talking, but not to forget. There are things which are not said for a very long time, but once they are said they are constantly repeated.

And so our life went on for four months of strained relationships, sometimes delightful, never completely open, in which some pleasure could still be found but from which all the charm had gone. Ellenore, however, grew no less attached to me. After our most violent quarrels she was just as anxious to see me and arranged the times of our meetings just as carefully as if ours were the most tender and peaceful union. I have often thought that my own behaviour helped to keep Ellenore in this frame of mind. Had I loved her as she loved me she would have been more controlled and considered the dangers she was flouting. But prudence was anathema to her because prudence came from me; she did not count the sacrifices she was making because she was bent on making me accept them; there was no time for her feelings towards me to cool because all her time and energy were devoted to maintaining her hold on me. The new date for my departure was drawing near, and the thought filled me with mingled pleasure and regret, like a man feels when he has to buy an infallible cure at the cost of a painful operation.

One morning Ellenore wrote asking me to go and see her at once. 'The Count,' she said, 'has forbidden me to see you: I refuse to obey this tyrannical order. I followed that man into exile, saved him from ruin, furthered all his interests. He can do without me now, but I cannot do without you.' It is easy to imagine the arguments I used to dissuade her from a scheme that struck me as unthinkable. I mentioned public opinion. 'Public opinion,' she replied, 'has never shown any justice to me. For ten years I have fulfilled all my obligations better than any wife, but that has not prevented public opinion from denying me my rightful position.' I reminded her of her children. 'My children also belong to M. de P—. He has recognized them and he will look after them. They will be only too fortunate to forget a mother who has nothing to share with them but her shame.' I redoubled my entreaties. 'Listen,' she said, 'if I break with the Count, are you going to refuse to see me? Are you?' she repeated, gripping my arm so roughly that I flinched. 'No, of course not,' I answered, 'and the greater your misfortune the more devoted I shall be. But do consider ...' 'Everything has been considered,' she broke in; 'but he is coming back, you must go now, and don't come here again.'

I spent the rest of that day in a state of unspeakable

torment. Two days went by with no news of Ellenore. It was agony not to know her fate and agony not to see her, and I was astonished at the pain this deprivation inflicted upon me. Yet I hoped she would have given up a decision I feared so much on her behalf, and I was beginning to persuade myself that she had done so when a letter was handed to me by a woman. In it Ellenore asked me to go and see her on the third floor of a certain house in a certain street. I hurried there, still hoping that as she could not receive me at M. de P—'s house she had wanted to see me elsewhere for the last time. But I found her settling in for a long stay. She came up to me, looking both happy and nervous, and trying to read in my eyes what my impression was. 'It is all broken off,' she said, 'and I am perfectly free. I have an income of my own of seventy-five louis, and that is enough for me. You are staying here six more weeks. When you go perhaps I can come to you, or perhaps you can come back and see me.' And as though dreading a reply she plunged into a mass of detail about her plans. She tried all manner of ways to convince me that she was going to be happy, that she had given up nothing for me and that the course she had decided upon suited her apart altogether from me. She was clearly making a great effort and only half believing what she was saying, intoxicating herself with words so as not to hear mine, spinning out what she was saying so as to put off the moment when my objections would plunge her back into despair. I could not find it in me to raise a single one, but accepted her sacrifice with thanks, saying how happy it made me; I even went much further and assured her that I had always hoped that an irrevocable determination would make it my duty never to leave her. I ascribed my hesitations to delicacy over agreeing with what must mean her ruin. In a word, I had no other thought than to dispel from her mind any pain, fear, regret, or uncertainty about my feelings. While I was saying all this I was not contemplating anything beyond that object, and I was sincere in my promises.

Chapter Five

Iт was not difficult to foresee the effect in society of the separation of Ellenore and Count P—. In a single moment Ellenore lost the fruit of ten years' devotion and loyalty, and no distinction was made between her and all the other women of her class who shamelessly indulge in a thousand successive affairs. For leaving her children she was regarded as an unnatural mother, and women of unimpeachable reputation repeated with relish that neglect of the one virtue essential to their sex soon spread to all the others. At the same time people pitied her so as not to forgo the pleasure of blaming me. My conduct was seen as that of a seducer, lacking in all sense of gratitude, who had violated the laws of hospitality and, to satisfy a passing whim, had sacrificed the peace of two people, one of whom he should have treated with respect and the other with consideration. A few of my father's friends made serious representations, others, less straightforward, made their displeasure felt by devious insinuations. Younger men, however, were delighted with the skill with which I had supplanted the Count and, with numerous witticisms that I tried in vain to discourage, congratulated me on my conquest and undertook to imitate me. I cannot describe how both this harsh criticism and humiliating praise hurt me. I am convinced that if I had really loved Ellenore I should have turned public opinion in our favour, for such is the strength of a true feeling that false interpretations and artificial conventions fall silent when it speaks. But I was an ordinary weak man, both grateful and enslaved, not driven by any motive power from the heart. And so I hedged in confusion, tried to cut conversations short, and if they went on ended them with sharp words that made it clear I was in a mood to pick a quarrel. Indeed I would much rather have fought people than have answered their questions.

Ellenore soon realized that opinion was turning against her. Two of M. de P—'s women relatives, whom he had forced to be friendly with her, now broke off the connexion with the greatest possible ostentation, delighted to give vent to the spite they had had to conceal for so long beneath the austere principles of morality. Men still saw her, but there crept into their tone a certain familiarity which showed that she no longer had an influential protector behind her, nor was vindicated by an almost official union. Some of them came because, after all, they had known her for years, others because she was still attractive and her recent frailty had given them aspirations they made no effort to disguise. They all found reasons for their connexion with her, which meant that each of them thought the connexion needed some justification. And so the unfortunate Ellenore found herself sunk down for ever into the position she had spent her life trying to rise out of. Everything conspired to bruise her soul and wound her pride. Being dropped by some seemed a proof of their contempt, being taken up by others a sign of some insulting hope. Solitude made her miserable, social life made her ashamed. No doubt I should have consoled her by clasping her to my heart and saying: 'Let us live only for one another and forget people who do not wish to know us, let us be happy in our respect for each other and our love alone!' And indeed I tried to do so, but when it comes to reviving a dying love what is the good of determination aroused by a sense of duty?

Neither Ellenore nor I was frank with the other. She dared not confide her worries to me, for they were the outcome of a sacrifice she knew very well I had never asked of her. I had accepted that sacrifice, and I dared not complain of a misfortune I had foreseen but had not had the strength to forestall. And so we never mentioned the only thing always in our minds. We lavished caresses upon each other and talked of love, but we talked of love for fear of talking about something else.

The moment some secret exists between two loving hearts, the moment one of them can decide to conceal one single thought from the other, the spell is broken and the bliss destroyed. Anger, injustice, even wandering affections can be put right again, but dissimulation brings into love a foreign element which perverts and withers it even in its own eyes.

By a strange inconsistency, while I was most indignantly repudiating the slightest insinuation against Ellenore, my general conversation was helping to do her harm. I had submitted to her will, but at the same time developed a horror of the domination of women. I was constantly inveighing against their fickleness, their tyranny, their exacting exhibitions of grief. I made a display of the harshest principles, and the very man who could not stand up against a tear, who gave in before melancholy silence, whose absences were haunted by the vision of the pain he had caused, showed himself scornful and merciless in everything he said. All my direct praises of Ellenore could not dispel the impression such talk produced. People detested me and pitied her, but they did not respect her. They criticized her for not having inspired in her lover more consideration for her sex and more respect for the ties of love.

One of Ellenore's regular visitors, who since her break with Count P— had shown the strongest passion for her, was so tactless in his pursuit of her that she was obliged to refuse to see him again. This man then indulged in insulting jokes about her which I felt I could not let pass. We fought, and

I wounded him seriously and was wounded myself. I could never describe the mingled anxiety, terror, gratitude, and love on Ellenore's face when she saw me after this incident. In spite of my entreaties she took up her abode with me and never left me for a moment until my recovery, reading to me by day and sitting up with me most of the night. She watched my slightest movement and anticipated my every wish, and her resourceful kindness sharpened her intelligence and doubled her strength. Over and over again she assured me that she would never have survived me, and I was overcome by affection and torn by remorse. I wished I could have found in myself the wherewithal to reward such faithful and tender attachment, and I called upon memories, imagination, and even reason and sense of duty, but all in vain. The difficulty of the situation and certainty that the future would separate us, and possibly some kind of revolt against a tie I could not break, were tormenting me. I blamed myself for the very ingratitude I was striving to hide from her. I was hurt when she appeared to question a love so necessary to her, but no less hurt when she appeared to believe in it. I felt she was a better person than I was and despised myself for being unworthy of her. It is a dreadful misfortune not to be loved when we are in love, but it is a very great one to be loved passionately when we have ceased to love. I had risked my life for Ellenore, but I would have given it a thousand times over to make her happy without me.

The six months allowed by my father had expired; I had to think about going. Ellenore did not object to my departure, nor even try to delay it, but she made me promise that I would come back to her in two months or else let her join me; I solemnly swore it should be so. What undertaking would I not have entered into at a time when I could see her fighting against herself and controlling her grief? She could have insisted on my not leaving her, and I knew in my heart that her tears would not have been disobeyed. I was grateful to her for not using her power; it seemed to make me love her the more. And it was only with the keenest regret that I was tearing myself away from one so exclusively devoted to me. There is something so deep in attachments of long standing. Without our realizing they become such an intimate part of our existence. At a distance and in cold blood we resolve to break them, and we think we are impatiently waiting for the moment to carry out the resolution, but when that moment comes it fills us with terror. Such is the strangeness of our unhappy nature that it is heartrending to leave somebody we have been finding no pleasure in staying with.

While I was away I wrote regularly to Ellenore. I was torn between fear that my letters might give her pain and desire to describe only the emotions I was feeling. I would have liked her to see through me, but see through me without being hurt, and so I was pleased with myself when I had managed to substitute for the word love the terms affection, friendship, or devotion. But then I would suddenly visualize poor Ellenore, sad and lonely with nothing to console her except my letters, and after two coldly thought-out pages would hurriedly add a few impassioned or tender sentences calculated to deceive her afresh. In this way, without saying enough to satisfy her I always said enough to mislead her. What a strange kind of deceit whose very success turned against me, prolonged my agony and was altogether unendurable!

I anxiously counted the days and hours and mentally tried to delay the passage of time, for the approaching moment when I should have to fulfil my promise filled me with foreboding. I could not think of any pretext for getting away, nor could I find any means whereby Ellenore could come and settle in the same town with me. Perhaps – I must be honest – perhaps I did not want such a thing to happen. I compared my quiet, independent life with the life of upheavals, worries and troubles to which passion condemned me. It was so pleasant to be free to come and go, set off and return without anybody paying the slightest attention. After the exhaustion of her love I was, as it were, finding rest in the indifference of others.

But I dared not let Ellenore suspect that I should have liked to abandon our scheme. She had gathered from my letters that it would be difficult for me to leave my father and wrote to me that in consequence she was beginning preparations for her departure. For a long time I did not oppose her decision, but avoided giving her a precise answer on this point. I vaguely indicated that I would always be delighted to know – and then I added, to make – her happy. What miserable ambiguities, what tortuous language! I deplored its obscurity but dreaded making it any clearer. At length I made up my mind to express myself openly, telling myself that I must, stirring up my conscience against my own weakness, strengthening my resolution with the thought of her peace of mind in order to keep the vision of her grief at bay. I strode up and down my room rehearsing aloud what I intended to say. But scarcely had I written a few lines before my mood changed: I was no longer considering the meaning my words must convey but the effect they could not fail to produce, and, my hand being controlled against my will as if by some supernatural power, all I did was advise her to wait for a few months. I had not said what was in my mind. My letter showed no signs of sincerity. The arguments I invented were feeble because they were not the genuine ones.

Ellenore's answer was passionate: she was outraged at my desire not to see her. What was she asking for? To live near me without anyone's knowledge. What had I to fear from her presence in a secret retreat in the depths of a big city where nobody knew her? She had given up everything for me, her fortune, her children, her good name, and she asked for nothing in return but to wait for me like a humble slave, spend a few minutes with me each day, enjoy the moments I could spare her. She had resigned herself to a separation of two months, not that she thought it was necessary but because it seemed to be my wish, and now that by dint of wearily piling day upon day she had reached the date I prescribed, I was suggesting that she should start the long ordeal all over again! She might have made a mistake, she might have entrusted her life to a hard, soulless man; I was in command of my own actions, but I was not in a position to command her to suffer, thrown over by the man for whom she had left everything.

Ellenore quickly followed this letter in person and let me know she had arrived. I went to her with the firm resolve to show great joy. I was eager to reassure her anxious heart and give her at least momentary peace and happiness. But she had been hurt, and in her mistrust she observed me closely and soon became aware of the efforts I was making, and she inflamed my pride with her reproaches and outrageously criticized my character. She drew such a picture of my despicable weakness that she made me more disgusted with her than with myself. An insane rage took possession of us, we gave up every word of mitigation and forgot every delicacy. It was as though Furies were driving us at each other. All that the most implacable hatred had invented about us we now applied to one another, and the two wretched creatures who alone in the world knew each other and alone were capable of doing each other justice, of understanding and consoling each other, now seemed to be irreconcilable enemies bent on mutual destruction.

We separated after a scene lasting three hours, and for the first time in our lives left each other with no explanation, no attempt to make amends. Scarcely was I away from Ellenore than my anger gave way to profound grief. I was in a kind of stupor, quite dazed by what had happened. I repeated my own words in amazement, found my own behaviour incomprehensible and tried to discover in myself what could have upset my reason.

It was very late and I dared not return to Ellenore. I made up my mind to see her first thing in the morning and went home to my father's. There was a good deal of company, and in such a crowd of people it was easy for me to keep in the background and hide my agitation. When we were left alone together he said: 'I am told that Count P—'s former mistress is in the town. I have always left you perfectly free and have never sought to know anything about your love affairs, but it does not look right for you to have an acknowledged mistress at your age, and I give you warning that I have taken steps to make her leave.' With these words he went out. I ran after him right as far as his room, but he waved me away. 'Father,' I said, 'God knows I did not make Ellenore come here, and God knows I want her to be happy, and to make her so I would agree never to see her again. But mind what you are doing. Thinking to separate me from her you might well bind me to her for ever.'

I sent at once for a manservant who had been with me on my travels and who knew all about my relations with Ellenore. I told him to find out at once, if it could possibly be done, what these steps were that my father had referred to. He was back in two hours. My father's secretary had disclosed in strict confidence that Ellenore was to receive an order to leave on the following day. 'Ellenore sent away!' I cried, 'Ellenore sent packing ignominiously! She came here for my sake alone, and I have broken her heart, I have cruelly watched her tears flow! Where could the unhappy creature lay her head, alone and wandering in a world which despises her and through my fault? To whom could she confide her sorrows?' I soon made up my mind what to do, won over the servant with money and promises and ordered a post-chaise for six in the morning at the town gates. I thought out a thousand plans for my eternal union with Ellenore; my whole heart had turned back to her and I was more in love with her than ever before. I was proud to give her my protection, eager to hold her in my arms, passion had flooded back into my soul and I was in a fever of mind, heart and senses that transformed my whole life. Had Ellenore wanted to leave me at that moment I should have died at her feet trying to prevent her.

Daylight came. I rushed to Ellenore. She was in bed and had been weeping all night; her eyes were still moist and her hair disarranged. She was astonished to see me. 'Come,' I said, 'we must go.' She tried to demur. 'Let us be going,' I went on. 'Have you anybody on earth to look after you and love you? Are not my arms your only refuge?' She still resisted. 'I have urgent reasons, as they concern me personally. In heaven's name come with me.' I dragged her away. On the journey I smothered her with kisses, held her close to my heart and only answered her questions with embraces. Finally I told her that having realized that my father meant to separate us I had felt I could not be happy without her, that I wanted to devote my life to her and unite us by every kind of tie. At first she was overcome with gratitude, but soon she discovered contradictions in my story. By her persistence she got the truth out of me; her joy vanished and her face clouded over.

'Adolphe,' she said, 'you are deceiving yourself; you are chivalrous and devoting yourself to me because I am being persecuted. You think what you feel is love, but it is only pity.' Why did she utter those fatal words? Why did she reveal a secret I did not want to know? I made efforts to reassure her, and I may possibly have succeeded, but the truth had flashed through my soul and the impulse had been destroyed. I was set on my sacrifice, but that did not make me any happier, and already a thought had sprung to my mind which once again I was reduced to concealing.

Chapter Six

WHEN we reached the frontier I wrote to my father. My letter was respectful but not without an undertone of bitterness. I resented his having tightened my bonds whilst claiming to break them. I told him that I would only leave Ellenore when she was properly settled and no longer in need of me, and begged him not to persecute her, and by so doing force me to remain tied to her for ever. I waited for his answer before deciding what way of life to adopt. His reply was: 'You are twenty-four, and I am not going to have recourse to an authority which is almost at an end and which in any case I have never used. I will even conceal your strange behaviour to the best of my ability, and spread it abroad that you went off on my orders and on business of mine. I will contribute generously to your expenses. You will soon realize yourself that the life you are leading is not the one you were made for. Your birth, talents, and fortune destined you for a different position in the world from that of follower of a woman with no settled home or position. Already your letter shows me that you are not pleased with yourself. Do reflect that nothing is to be gained by prolonging a situation one is ashamed of. You are using up the best years of your youth to no purpose, and such a loss is irreparable.'

My father's letter was like a knife stabbing me over and over again. What he was now saying I had already told myself a hundred times, and a hundred times I had felt ashamed of wasting my life in obscurity and inaction. I would have preferred reproaches and threats: I would have taken pride in standing up to him and felt it was necessary to muster my strength and defend Ellenore from any perils that might assail her. But there were no perils; I was being left perfectly free, and this freedom only made me the less patient in bearing a burden apparently of my own choosing.

We settled in Caden, a little town in Bohemia. I continually told myself that since I had made Ellenore's fate my responsibility I must not make her unhappy. So I managed to control myself, and kept even the tiniest signs of dissatisfaction locked in my heart, calling upon all the resources of my mind to create an artificial gaiety to conceal my profound melancholy. This effort had an unhoped-for effect upon me. We are such unstable creatures that feelings we pretend to have we really do have in the end. I found myself half forgetting the resentments I was concealing. My everlasting witticisms dispelled my own melancholy, and the assurances of affection I kept making to Ellenore filled my heart with an agreeable emotion almost like love itself.

At times I was haunted by unwelcome memories. When I was alone I indulged in fits of anxiety and conceived countless strange plans to break loose from an environment in which I was out of place. But I thrust these impressions away like bad dreams. Ellenore seemed happy; could I possibly disturb her happiness? Nearly five months went by in this way.

One day I noticed that Ellenore was in a very emotional state and trying not to tell me something that was on her mind. After long pleadings she made me promise not to oppose a decision she had come to, and then admitted that M. de P— had written to her. His lawsuit had been successful; he remembered with gratitude the services she had rendered him in their ten years together. He offered her half his fortune, not indeed to have her back with him, for that was no longer possible, but on condition that she left the ungrateful and perfidious man who had come between them.

'I have answered him,' she said, 'and as you can guess, I have refused.' I guessed all too well. I was touched, but horrified at the fresh sacrifice Ellenore was making for me. But I dared not raise any objection, for my attempts in that direction had always been so fruitless. I went away to think over the line I should take. I saw clearly that our connexion would have to be severed; it was irksome to me and becoming harmful to her. I was the only obstacle between her and recovery of a respected position and that consideration which in society sooner or later results from wealth. I was the only barrier between her and her children – in fact in my own eyes I had no excuses left. In these circumstances to let her have her own way ceased to be generosity and became culpable weakness. I had promised my father to recover my freedom as soon as I was no longer necessary to Ellenore. And indeed it was time I embarked upon a career, began to lead an active life, to acquire some claim to the respect of men and used my abilities for some worthy purpose. And so I went back to Ellenore, thinking I was unshakeable in my determination to force her not to reject the Count's offer and, if need be, declare my love for her was dead. 'My dear,' I said, 'we can struggle on for a time against our destiny, but in the end it has to be accepted. The laws of society are stronger than the will of men; the most compelling emotions dash themselves to pieces against the fatality of circumstances. We insist upon listening to our hearts alone, but in vain; sooner or later we are constrained to listen to reason. I cannot go on keeping you in a situation as humiliating for you as for me. I cannot do this for your sake or mine.' While I was speaking, without looking at Ellenore, I could feel my ideas getting more and more confused and my resolution weakening. Wishing to recover my strength of purpose I hurried on: 'I shall always be your friend and always have the deepest affection for you. The two years we have had together will never fade from my memory, and will always remain the finest time of my life. But love, that ecstasy of the senses, that unsought-for madness, that forgetting of all one's interests and duties, this, Ellenore, has gone.' For a long time I waited for her answer without raising my eyes to look at her. When at length I did look up she was motionless, gazing at all the things around her but seeing nothing. I took her hand; it felt frozen. 'What do you expect me to do?' she said, avoiding my touch. 'Am I not alone, alone in the universe, alone without a soul to understand? What else have you to say? Haven't you said it all? Isn't everything over, finished beyond recall? Leave me alone, go away, isn't that what you want?' She made as if to leave me, but staggered. I tried to hold her, but she fell senseless at my feet. I raised her up, kissed her, and brought her back to consciousness. 'Ellenore,' I cried, 'come back, back to yourself and me. I love you with true love, with the most tender love, I was lying to you so as to leave you a free choice.' How inexplicable is the credulity of the heart! These simple words, belied by so many previous ones, gave her back life and confidence; she made me repeat them several times and seemed to breathe them in hungrily. She believed me: she gave herself up to the intoxication of her own love, taking it for ours. Her reply to Count P— was confirmed, and I was more deeply involved than ever.

Three months later there opened up a new possibility of a change in Ellenore's circumstances. By one of those vicissitudes so common in republics torn by party politics her father was recalled to Poland and his wealth restored. Although he hardly knew his daughter, who had been taken to France by her mother at the age of three, he wanted to have her to live with him. Only the vaguest rumours about

Ellenore's adventures had reached him in Russia, where he had lived throughout his exile. Ellenore was his only child, he was afraid of loneliness and anxious to be looked after and so his sole care was to find out his daughter's whereabouts, and as soon as he had done so he strongly urged her to go and live with him. She could not have any real fondness for a father she did not remember having seen, but she felt it her duty to obey, for by so doing she would secure a large fortune for her children and regain the social position she had been deprived of by her misfortunes and behaviour. But she declared categorically that she would not go to Poland unless I went with her. 'I am no longer at the age when the spirit opens to receive new impressions,' she said. 'My father is a stranger to me, and if I stay here others will eagerly surround him and he will be just as happy. My children will have M. de P—'s money. I realize that I shall be blamed by all; I shall be considered an ungrateful daughter and a callous mother. But I have gone through too much, and I am no longer young enough to be greatly impressed by public opinion. If my decision is somewhat heartless, you must blame yourself, Adolphe. If I could entertain any illusions about you I might agree to our parting for a time, and the bitterness of our separation would be mitigated by the prospect of a happy and lasting reunion; but you would be only too glad to think I was two hundred leagues away, happy and peaceful, in the bosom of my family and surrounded by luxury. You would write me sensible letters on the subject – I can see them now – and they would break my heart; I refuse to run that risk. Not for me the consolation of telling myself that by dint of sacrificing my whole life I have succeeded in inspiring an attachment worthy of me. Nevertheless you have accepted this sacrifice. Already your distant manner and the formality of our relationship are causing me suffering enough. I passively accept such sufferings as you inflict upon me, but I refuse to face self-inflicted ones.'

There was a sharp and violent tone in her voice which betokened firm determination rather than deep or touching emotion. For some time she had been showing irritation even while asking me for things, as though I had already refused them. She could make me do whatever she liked, but she knew that what I did was belied by what I thought. She would have liked to penetrate into the innermost shrine of my thoughts and break down the sullen resistance which angered her. I mentioned my circumstances, my father's wishes, my own desire, I begged and stormed, but she was unshakeable. I tried to rekindle her generosity, just as though love were not the most self-centred of all passions, and consequently the least generous when flouted. I had the fantastic idea of trying to touch her heart by the unhappy plight I was in through remaining with her, but I only succeeded in exasperating her. I promised to go and see her in Poland, but she only read into my reserved and guarded promises my impatience to get away from her.

The first year of our stay in Caden had come to an end without there being any change in our situation. Whenever Ellenore found me moody or depressed she began by being distressed, then took offence and by her recriminations dragged from me an admission of the weariness I would have liked to conceal. For my part, if Ellenore seemed to be happy I was annoyed to see her enjoying a state of affairs that was costing me my own happiness, and I upset her brief enjoyment by insinuations which enlightened her about my inner feelings. And so we took turns at attacking each other with indirect remarks, only to retreat afterwards into general protestations and vague self-justification, finally relapsing into silence. For we were each so perfectly aware of what the other was on the point of saying that we both kept quiet in order not to have to hear it. Sometimes one of us was ready to give way, but we missed the right moment for reconciliation. Our mistrustful and wounded hearts were no longer in harmony.

I often wondered why I stayed on in such an irksome position, and told myself that it was because Ellenore would follow me if I ran away, and that would involve yet another sacrifice. But I decided that I must humour her one last time, for she could make no further demands on me once I had returned her to her own family circle. I was just about to suggest going with her to Poland when she received news that her father had died suddenly. He had made her his sole heir, but his will was contradicted by letters of a later date that some distant relations were threatening to use to their advantage. Although for a long time she had not had much to do with her father, Ellenore was grief-stricken by his death, and reproached herself for having abandoned him. Soon she put the blame for this on me. 'You have made me fail in a sacred duty. Now nothing is involved except my money, and I will sacrifice that for you even more willingly. But I am certainly not going on my own to a country where I shall find nothing but enemies.' 'I have never sought,' I answered, 'to make you fail in any duty, but I confess that I should have liked you to deign to consider that I also was finding it painful to be failing in mine. I have not managed to get you to do me this much justice. Very well, I give in, Ellenore; your interests overrule every other consideration. We will set off together whenever you like.'

And we did indeed set off. The things of interest on the journey and their novelty, with the efforts we made to keep ourselves under control, did from time to time bring back some remnants of affection. Our long familiarity with each other's character and the varied circumstances we had come through together had given our every word, almost our every movement, memories which suddenly carried us back into the past and filled us with an involuntary tenderness as lightning flashes through the night but does not dispel it. We were living, so to speak, on a sort of memory of the heart, strong enough to make the thought of separation painful, but too weak for us to find satisfaction in being together. I indulged in these emotions as a relaxation from my normal tension. I would have liked to give Ellenore tokens of my love that would have made her happy, and indeed I sometimes went back to the language of love, but these emotions and this language resembled the pale and faded leaves which, like remains of funeral wreaths, grow listlessly on the branches of an uprooted tree.

Chapter Seven

As soon as she arrived Ellenore was granted permission to assume full enjoyment of the disputed estate on condition that she would not dispose of anything until the case had been settled. She took up residence in one of her father's properties. My own father, who never broached any subject directly in his letters, confined himself to filling them with insinuations against my journey. For example: 'You told me you were not going; you had developed at great length all your reasons for not going. Consequently I was perfectly sure you would go. I can only feel pity that with your spirit of independence you invariably do what you do not want to do. Not that I can pass judgement on a situation with which I am only partially acquainted. Until now you have been, as far as I could see, Ellenore's protector, and in that relationship there was something chivalrous in your behaviour which did honour to your character, whatever the person to whom you were attached. But today your relationship is not the same at all; it is no longer you who are keeping her, but she you; you are living in her house, a stranger she is bringing into her family. I make no comment upon a position that is your own choice, but as it may have some drawbacks for you I would like to attenuate them as far as it lies within my power. I am writing a letter of recommendation to Baron T—, our minister in the country where you now are. I do not know whether it will suit you to use this recommendation, but there is no need to read into it anything more than a proof of my desire to help – not a threat to the independence you have always managed to defend so successfully against your father.'

I stifled the thoughts that this kind of style inspired. The estate where I was living with Ellenore was quite near Warsaw, so I went into the city and saw Baron T—. He welcomed me kindly, asked the reason for my stay in Poland and what my plans were. I was not too sure how to answer. After a few minutes of embarrassed conversation he said: 'I am going to be frank with you. I know the motives that have brought you to this country – your father has written to me. I might even say that I sympathize with them, for indeed there is no man alive who has not once in his life been torn between desire to break off an unsuitable affair and fear of hurting a woman he once loved. In their inexperience young men greatly exaggerate the difficulties of such a situation; they like to believe in the genuinenesss of all those exhibitions of grief which the weak and passionate sex uses as a substitute for all the weapons of strength and reason. The heart is wounded, but self-esteem is flattered, and a young man who in all good faith thinks he is yielding to the despair of which he is the cause is in reality only sacrificing himself to the illusions of his own vanity. Not one of the passionate women of whom the world is full has not protested that she would die if abandoned, but every single one of them is still alive and has found consolation.' I made as if to interrupt. 'Forgive me, my young friend,' he went on, 'if I am not expressing myself with sufficient tact, but the good reports I have had of you, the talents you clearly possess and the career you ought to take up, lay upon me an obligation to hold nothing back. I can read your soul in spite of you and better than you can yourself; you are no longer in love with the woman who is dominating you and dragging you in her wake, for if you still were you would not have come to see me. You knew your father had written to me and it was easy for you to foresee what I had to say to you; you have not been sorry to hear from my mouth arguments you are constantly going over in your own mind, and always fruitlessly. Ellenore's reputation is far from being spotless ...' 'Please let us put an end to a pointless conversation,' I broke in. 'Ellenore's early years may have been shaped by unhappy circumstances, and deceptive appearances may give rise to harsh judgements. But I have known her for three years now, and a loftier soul, a nobler character, and a purer and more generous heart cannot be found on this earth.' 'That may well be,' he replied, 'but public opinion does not go into fine distinctions of that kind. The facts are clear and public property. Do you think that by preventing my referring to them you can destroy them? Look here, in this world we must know what we want. You are not going to marry Ellenore?' 'No, I don't think so,' I exclaimed, 'she has never wanted that herself.' 'Then what do you propose to do? She is ten years older than you, and you are twenty-six; you will look after her another ten years and she will be old whilst you will have reached the prime of life with nothing satisfying either begun or finished. You will be given up to boredom and she to ill-temper; each day you will find her less attractive and each day she will find you more necessary. And the total result of your illustrious birth, brilliant fortune, and superior intellect will be your vegetating somewhere in Poland, forgotten by your friends, lost to fame and tormented by a woman who will never be pleased with you, whatever you do. I will add only one word more and we will never again refer to this embarrasing subject. All careers are open to you: literature, the army, administration, and you can aspire to the most brilliant of marriages, you are born to succeed in any direction, but you must bear in mind that between you and all kinds of success there is an insuperable obstacle, and this obstacle is Ellenore.' 'Sir,' I answered, 'I felt I owed it to you to hear you in silence, but I also owe it to myself to declare that you have not shaken me. I must repeat that nobody can judge Ellenore but myself; nobody else fully recognizes the genuineness of her feelings and the depth of her emotions. As long as she needs me I shall stay by her side. No success could console me for leaving her in misery, and if I had to confine my whole career to rendering her assistance, upholding her in her tribulations, surrounding her with my protecting love against the injustices of prejudiced public opinion, I should not think I had spent my life in vain.'

I went out as I finished this speech. But who can explain what instability made the sentiment that was dictating it perish before I had even finished saying the words? I deliberately set out to return on foot so as to put off the moment of seeing this very Ellenore I had just been defending, and I hurried through the town in my eagerness to be alone.

When I reached open country I slackened my pace, and countless thoughts crowded in upon me. The fateful words: 'Between you and all kinds of success there is an insuperable obstacle, and this obstacle is Ellenore,' echoed all round me. I looked back long and wistfully over the time that had gone by, never to return, recalling the hopes of my youth, the confidence with which I had once thought I could command the future, the praises that greeted my earliest ventures, the dawning of a reputation I had seen brighten and then fade away. I went over the names of many of my fellow students whom I had treated with lofty disdain but who, simply by sticking to work and living a regular life, had now left me far behind on the road to fortune, prestige and glory, and my own inaction weighed heavily on me. As misers conjure up in the treasures they have amassed all the goods those treasures could buy, so I saw in Ellenore deprivation of all the successes I might have expected. It was not just one career I mourned; as I had never tried any career I mourned them all. Never having put my talents to the test, I imagined they were limitless and cursed them because of it, wishing nature had made me weak and commonplace, and spared me at any rate the remorse that comes from deliberate self-abasement. Any praise or approval of my intelligence or knowledge seemed an unbearable reproach, like hearing admiration for the powerful arms of an athlete chained down in a dungeon. Whenever I made a bid to regain my courage and tell myself that the time for action was not yet past, the vision of Ellenore rose up before me like a ghost and thrust me back into the void. I fell into fits of rage against her, but in some oddly confused way these rages did nothing to lessen my terror at the thought of hurting her.

Exhausted by these bitter emotions, my soul suddenly tried to find refuge in opposite ones. A few words dropped casually by Baron T— about the possibility of my finding happiness and tranquillity in marriage helped to build up in my mind the ideal wife. I mused on the peace, the honourable position, and even independence such an outcome would provide, for the fetters with which I had been hampered for so long made me a thousand times more dependent than an official, accepted union could ever have done. I imagined my father's joy; I felt a keen impatience to resume my rightful place in my own country and among my equals; I saw myself balancing austere and irreproachable behaviour against all the things alleged about me by the coldly or frivolously spiteful and all the criticisms heaped upon me by Ellenore.

'She continually accuses me of being hard, ungrateful, pitiless. Ah, if Heaven had vouchsafed me a partner whom social conventions had allowed me to acknowledge and my father would not have been ashamed to accept as a daughter, I should have been a thousand times happier in making her happy. These feelings of mine are now being disparaged because they are hurt and suffering. These feelings are being peremptorily ordered to manifest themselves in demonstrations which my heart refuses to concede to scenes and threats, how lovely it would be to indulge them with a woman I loved and who shared with me a regular and respected way of life! What have I not done for Ellenore? For her I left my country and family, for her I have inflicted grief upon my aged father who even now is sorrowing far away, for her I am living in this place where my youth is flying by in solitude, without fame, honour, or pleasure. Are not all these sacrifices, made without duty or love, a proof of what love and duty could make me do? If I am so afraid of the sorrow of a woman who only dominates me by her sorrow, what care I should give to removing every affliction, every pain from the life of the woman I could openly devote myself to, without regrets or reservations! How different I should appear from what I am now! How swiftly I should see the end of this bitterness which I am now being blamed for because its origin is unknown! How grateful I should be to Heaven and how well disposed towards men!'

So I told myself; my eyes filled with tears as a thousand memories flooded back into my soul. My relationship with Ellenore had poisoned all these memories for me. Everything that reminded me of my childhood, the scenes amongst which my earliest years had been spent, the companions in my first games, the elderly relations who had lavished upon me the first tokens of their interest, all these things wounded and tortured me, and I was forced to thrust aside the most delectable visions and natural aspirations as if they were guilty thoughts. On the other hand the wife suddenly conjured up by my imagination fitted into all these visions and made all such wishes permissible; she was identified with all my duties, pleasures, tastes, she linked my present life with that phase of my youth when hope opened out before me such a vast prospect, that period from which Ellenore separated me like a chasm. The minutest details and tiniest things came back clearly into my mind: I could see the ancient castle where I had lived with my father, the surrounding woods and the river lapping against its walls, the mountains closing its horizon, and all these things seemed so real, so intensely alive that they made me tremble almost unbearably, and among them my imagination placed a young and innocent creature adorning them, animating them with hope. I wandered on, lost in this reverie and still with no plan in mind, not telling myself I must break with Ellenore, not even having anything more than a dim and confused impression of reality, and like a man broken by trouble, consoled in sleep by a dream, but foreseeing that the dream must have an end. Suddenly I saw Ellenore's house which I had been unconsciously approaching. I stopped short and then took another turning, glad to put off the moment of hearing her voice again.

Daylight was waning, the sky was still, the countryside was becoming deserted. Men were giving up their toil and were leaving nature to herself. Gradually my thoughts took on a more serious and portentous tone. In the ever deepening shades of night, in the great silence which enveloped me, broken only by an occasional distant sound, my agitation was succeeded by a calmer and more solemn frame of mind. I cast my eyes round the greyish horizon whose boundaries had faded from sight, and that in itself gave me a sense of limitless space. It was a long time since I had felt anything of the kind. Having been continually taken up in exclusively personal reflections, with my eyes always trained upon my own situation, I had become unfamiliar with general ideas; only concerned with Ellenore and myself – with Ellenore who inspired only pity mingled with weariness and with myself for whom I had ceased to have any respect – I had shrunk, as it were, into a new kind of self-centredness, one without courage, discontented and humiliated. And so it was with self-congratulation that I awoke once again to thoughts of another order and found I still had the ability to forget myself and devote my mind to impersonal meditation: my soul seemed to be emerging from a long and shameful abasement.

Almost the whole night passed in this way. I wandered on at random through fields, woods and hamlets where all was still. Now and again, in some distant dwelling, I saw a dim light piercing the darkness. 'Yonder,' I said to myself, 'some poor wretch may be struggling on in grief, or wrestling with death, death the inexplicable mystery men still seem unable to accept despite daily experience, the certain end which brings neither consolation nor peace, the subject of habitual unconcern and momentary panic! And I too,' I went on, 'am indulging in this same senseless inconsistency! I am rebelling against life as though life were never-ending! I am spreading misery around me so as to win back a few years of wretchedness that time will soon snatch away! Ah, enough of these useless struggles! Let me stand unmoved, a detached onlooker at an already half-spent existence; anybody can take it and tear it to pieces – they won't make it last any longer! Is it worth fighting over?'

The thought of death has always had great power over me. In my keenest afflictions it has always sufficed to calm me at once, and now it produced its usual effect upon my soul, and my feelings about Ellenore lost some of their bitterness. All my annoyance vanished, and all that remained of the impressions of this night of frenzy was a mild and almost tranquil emotion. Perhaps my physical weariness contributed to this tranquillity.

Dawn was at hand, and I could already make out objects in the landscape. I realized that I was a considerable distance from Ellenore's home. I pictured her anxiety and I was hurrying back to her as fast as my exhaustion would allow when I met a man on horseback whom she had sent to look for me. He told me that she had been intensely worried for the past twelve hours, that having been into Warsaw and all over the surrounding district she had returned in a state of indescribable distress and that the villagers had scoured the countryside in every direction in search of me. At first this story filled me with quite painful resentment. It was irritating to see myself subjected by Ellenore to such officious surveillance. It was useless to tell myself that it was due to nothing but her love, for was not her love also the cause of all my troubles? But I managed to overcome this feeling, which I was ashamed of. I knew she was alarmed and ill. I leaped on horseback and quickly covered the distance between us. She welcomed me with transports of joy. I was touched by her emotion. Our conversation was brief because it soon occurred to her that I must be in need of rest, and I left her, for once at any rate, without having said anything to grieve her.

Chapter Eight

I ROSE next day haunted by the same thoughts which had disturbed me the day before. My uneasiness increased during the following days. Ellenore tried in vain to find out the cause, but I answered her pressing questions in awkward monosyllables, stiffening myself against her insistence, knowing full well that frankness from me would mean sorrow for her and that her sorrow would force me into fresh dissimulation.

In her worried and bewildered state she sought the help of one of her women friends to discover the secret she accused me of hiding from her; eager to deceive herself she was looking for a fact where there was only a feeling. This friend spoke to me about my strange state, the care I was taking to discourage any idea of a lasting union, and my inexplicable desire to make a break and find solitude. I listened for a long time without a word; until that moment I had told nobody that I no longer loved Ellenore, for I shrank from putting into words what seemed to me a betrayal. Yet I wanted to justify myself, and so I told my story with circumspection, praising Ellenore highly, admitting the illogicality of my own behaviour but blaming it on to the difficulties of our situation, and not allowing myself one word which would state clearly that the real trouble was absence of love. She was touched by my story, seeing generosity in what I called weakness, misfortune in what I called hardness of heart. The very explanations which infuriated the passionate Ellenore carried conviction in the mind of her impartial friend. How fair we all are when we are not involved ourselves! Whoever you may be, never discuss with another the interests of your own heart; the heart alone can plead its own cause and plumb the depths of its own wounds. Any intermediary becomes a judge who analyses, comes to a compromise, realizes that indifference can exist, indeed allows it to be possible, recognizes it as inevitable, and hence excuses it. In this way indifference is amazed to find itself legitimized in its own eyes. Ellenore's reproaches had convinced me that I was guilty, but now I learned from the woman who thought she was defending her that I was merely unfortunate. I was led on to make a complete avowal of my feelings; I agreed that I felt devotion, sympathy, pity for Ellenore, but I added that love played no part in the duty I was imposing upon myself. This truth, until then kept locked in my heart, and only once or twice revealed to Ellenore under stress or in anger, assumed in my eyes more reality and strength from the mere fact of its having been confided to another. It is a major step, and an irreparable one, when we suddenly reveal to a third party the secret places of an intimate relationship; daylight, as it penetrates this sanctuary, shows up and completes the ravages that night had enveloped in its shadows. In the same way bodies buried in the tomb often preserve their pristine shape until the outer air strikes them and reduces them to dust.

Ellenore's friend left me. I do not know what account she gave of our conversation, but on my way to the drawing-room I heard Ellenore talking in very animated tones, and when she saw me she stopped. Soon she began expressing in devious ways certain general observations which were really nothing less than personal attacks. 'Nothing is more curious,' she said, 'than the zeal of certain sorts of friendship; there are people who officiously busy themselves with your interests the better to abandon your cause. They call it attachment: I would rather call it hatred.' I quickly gathered that

Ellenore's friend had championed my cause against her and had annoyed her by not seeming to think me guilty enough. Thus I felt I was in league with another against Ellenore, and that was one more barrier between our hearts.

A few days later Ellenore went further, for she was incapable of any self-control, and as soon as she thought she had grounds for complaint she made straight for an explanation with no beating about the bush, preferring the risk of a total break to the constraint of dissimulation. The two friends quarrelled and parted for ever.

'Why bring outsiders into our private discussions?' I said. 'Do we need a third party to help us come to an understanding? And if we lack that understanding what third party could remedy the situation?' 'You are right,' she answered, 'but it is all your fault; I used not to have to go to anybody else in order to reach your heart.'

Suddenly she announced that she proposed to change her way of life. I gathered from what she said that she ascribed my gnawing unhappiness to the isolation in which we were living. She was working through all the wrong explanations before resigning herself to the right one. We spent dull evenings alone together in silence or ill-humour, for the spring of our long conversations had dried up.

Ellenore therefore resolved to attract to her house members of aristocratic families living in or near Warsaw. It was easy to visualize the difficulties and dangers of these schemes of hers. The relatives who were challenging her right of inheritance had revealed the follies of her past and spread a thousand scandalous rumours. I trembled at the humiliations that she would have to face and tried to dissuade her from the idea. But my representations were unavailing, and I hurt her pride by my fears, although I only expressed them cautiously. She assumed that I was embarrassed by our relationship because her position was ambiguous, and that made her all the more eager to regain an honourable place in society. Her efforts were crowned with some success, for her fortune, her beauty, that time had so far only slightly dimmed, and even the stories of her adventures, in fact everything about her, aroused curiosity. She was soon surrounded by a large circle, but she was secretly a prey to embarrassment and anxiety. I was uncomfortable about my position and she imagined I was about hers, and so was trying to get out of it; but the strength of her desire left no room for tactful manoeuvre and the falseness of her position made her erratic in her behaviour and hasty in her moves. Her intelligence was acute but lacked breadth; moreover the acuteness of her mind was marred by the impulsiveness of her character whilst its lack of breadth prevented her from seeing the wisest course of action and grasping subtle distinctions. For the first time she had an aim in life, and by rushing at it she missed it. What sickening humiliations she had to swallow without revealing them to me! How many times I blushed for her without finding the strength to tell her! Such is the impression that reserve and moderation make upon people that I had seen her more respected by M. de P—'s friends when she was his mistress than she was by her neighbours as heiress to a great fortune and surrounded by vassals. Haughty and humble in turn, sometimes considerate but sometimes touchy, there was in her actions and words a kind of feverishness which is fatal to that prestige which only calm can give.

By picking out these faults of Ellenore I am accusing and condemning myself. A single word from me would have given her that calm. Why could I not say it?

And yet our life together was happier, for amusements gave us relief from our usual thoughts. We were alone only occasionally, and as we had unlimited confidence in each other, except in the matter of our intimate feelings, we substituted general remarks and statements of fact for such feelings, and our conversations recovered a certain charm. But soon this new way of life gave rise to a fresh perplexity for me. Lost in the crowd surrounding Ellenore, I noticed that I was looked upon as an object of astonishment and censure. The time was approaching for her case to be heard, and her opponents maintained that she had alienated her father's love by her numberless follies. My presence lent colour to these assertions, and her friends blamed me for doing her a disservice. They excused her passion for me but accused me of lack of delicacy, of taking advantage, as they put it, of a feeling I ought to have discouraged. I was the only one to know that if I left her I should have her following on my heels, and that in order to do so she would neglect any interest in her own fortune and abandon all the dictates of prudence. I could not share this secret with the world at large, and so all I could appear to be in Ellenore's home was a stranger inimical to the success of the very steps which were to decide her fate, and, by a strange reversal of the truth, while I was the victim of her unshakeable will she was being pitied as the victim of my hold over her.

A fresh circumstance now complicated this painful situation still further.

Ellenore's actions and behaviour suddenly underwent a strange transformation. Until then she had never seemed interested in anybody but me; suddenly I saw her accepting and provoking the attentions of the men around her. This woman, so reserved, so cold and quick to take offence, suddenly seemed to change character. She encouraged the affection and even hopes of a crowd of young men, some of whom were captivated by her beauty, whilst others, in spite of the errors of her past, seriously aspired to her hand. She let them have long conversations alone with her and her manner with them was ambiguous but attractive, discouraging but only gently, so as to hold them by suggesting indecision rather than indifference, and deferment rather than refusal. I learned from her later, and the facts showed it to be the case, that she was acting in this way from an ill-advised and deplorable piece of calculation. She thought she could revive my love by arousing my jealousy, but it was merely raking over ashes that nothing could rekindle. Possibly also, without her realizing it herself, there was some feminine vanity in it; she was hurt by my coolness and anxious to prove to herself that she was still attractive. Or it may even have been that in the loneliness of heart in which I had left her, she drew a kind of consolation from hearing others repeating expressions of love which I had long since abandoned.

At all events, I did misinterpret her motives for a time. I thought I saw a glimpse of my future freedom, and congratulated myself. For fear that some thoughtless impulse of mine might upset the course of this great crisis on which I counted for my liberation, I became more gentle in manner and seemed happier. Ellenore took my gentleness for affection, my hopes of seeing her at last happy without me for the desire to make her happy myself, and she congratulated herself on her subtlety. Yet she was sometimes perturbed that I seemed so unconcerned, and blamed me for putting no obstacles in the way of affairs which apparently threatened to take her from me. I turned these accusations aside with jokes but did not always succeed in calming her fears – her character showed through the dissimulation she had forced herself to adopt. The old scenes began again on different grounds, but they were no less stormy. Ellenore saw her own faults in me, and let me suspect that a single word from me would make her wholly mine again; then, offended by my silence, she threw herself once more into flirtations with a kind of frenzy.

It is at this point, I feel sure, that I shall be accused of weakness. I wanted to be free and I could have been with everybody's approval; perhaps, indeed, I should have been, for Ellenore's behaviour authorized me and seemed to be forcing me to free myself. But did I not know that this behaviour of hers was of my own making? Did I not know that in her heart she had never ceased to love me? Could I punish her for indiscretions I was making her commit, and with cold hypocrisy seek in those indiscretions a pretext for pitilessly abandoning her?

I really am not trying to make excuses, and I blame myself more bitterly than another might do in my place, but I can at least solemnly claim that I have never acted out of calculation, but have always been guided by genuine and natural feelings. How comes it that with such feelings I have for so long brought about nothing but my own misfortune and that of others?

But as they watched me people were puzzled. My living with Ellenore could only be explained by a deep attachment to her, but my indifference towards the relationships she always seemed ready to embark upon appeared to give the lie to any such attachment. My inexplicable tolerance was put down to lack of any strong principles, to a carelessness about morals characteristic, it was said, of a profoundly selfish man corrupted by the world. These conjectures, all the more likely to impress for being in keeping with the minds who made them, were accepted and repeated. The gossip finally reached my ears. I was outraged by this unexpected discovery. The reward for all I had done was scorn and calumny. For the sake of a woman I had given up all interests and thrust aside all the pleasures of life, and now I was the one to be condemned.

I remonstrated strongly with Ellenore. A single word from me sufficed and all this mob of admirers she had gathered round in order to make me afraid of losing her was sent packing. She limited her circle to a few ladies and a handful of elderly men. Everything appeared to return to a normal routine, but that only made us more unhappy still, for Ellenore thought she had established new claims upon me and I felt burdened with new chains.

I cannot describe all the bitterness and scenes that resulted from this further complicated relationship. Our existence was one perpetual storm; intimacy lost all its charms and love all its sweetness, and even those short-lived renewals which seem to heal incurable wounds for a few fleeting instants occurred no more. The truth showed through at every turn, and in order to make my meaning clear I resorted to the harshest and most pitiless expressions, never stopping until Ellenore was in tears, but her very tears were like molten lava falling drop by drop on to my heart, making me scream with pain, but not retract. It was at these times that more than once she rose to her feet, pale and prophetic. 'Adolphe,' she said, 'you don't know the harm you are doing. You will realize it one day, you will learn it from me when you have driven me into the grave.' Wretched creature that I am! When she spoke in this way why did I not hurl myself into the grave before her?

Chapter Nine

I HAD not been back to Baron T—'s house since my first visit. One morning I received this note from him:

The advice I gave you did not justify such a long absence. Whatever course you adopt over what is your own business, you are still the son of my best friend, and I shall not enjoy the pleasure of your company any the less. Moreover it will give me much pleasure to introduce you into a circle to which I venture to promise you will be very glad to belong. May I add that the more unusual your way of life (and far be it from me to disapprove), the more desirable it is for you to dispel doubtless unfounded prejudices by letting yourself be seen in society.

I was grateful for this kindness shown me by an older man. I called upon him; the subject of Ellenore was not raised. He kept me to dinner, and that day there were only a few men there, and they were witty and very pleasant. At first I felt ill at ease, but I made an effort, recovered my spirits, began talking and displayed as much brilliance and knowledge as was in my power. I noticed I was successful in winning approval. This kind of success gave me once again a certain satisfaction based on vanity which I had long been deprived of, and this satisfaction made Baron T—'s society still more enjoyable.

My visits became more frequent. He entrusted me with one or two tasks connected with his political mission, which he felt he could safely leave in my hands. Ellenore was at first surprised at this change in my way of life, but I told her about the Baron's friendship with my father, and how glad I was to be able to console the latter for my absence by appearing to be usefully occupied. Poor Ellenore, and I write this

.now with a feeling of remorse, poor Ellenore was happier because I seemed more settled, and she resigned herself without undue complaint to spending often a large part of the day apart from me. As for the Baron, once we had established a certain amount of confidence in each other he raised the subject of Ellenore again. My fixed intention was to speak well of her at all times, but without realizing it I was referring to her in freer and more detached terms, sometimes showing by my general remarks that I accepted the necessity of a separation, sometimes letting jokes come to my rescue and laughing about women and how hard it was to break with them. This kind of talk amused an elderly official whose passions were all spent, but who vaguely recollected that he too had been tormented by love-affairs when he was young. And so the very fact that I was hiding my feelings led to my more or less deceiving everybody. I was deceiving Ellenore because I knew that the Baron wanted to get me away and yet I kept it from her, and I was deceiving M. de T— because I let him hope that I was prepared to break my bonds. This duplicity was quite foreign to my normal character, but a man deteriorates as soon as he harbours a single thought that he is constantly obliged to conceal.

Until then I had met in the Baron's house only the men who made up his intimate circle. One day he suggested that I should stay for a grand reception he was giving in honour of his master's birthday. 'You will meet some of the most beautiful women in Poland,' he said. 'It is true that the woman you love will not be there, and I am sorry, but there are some women whom one only sees in their own homes.' This expression was a painful one for me, and I remained silent, but I was secretly reproaching myself for not defending Ellenore who, had anyone insulted me in her presence, would have come so readily to my defence.

It was a large gathering, and I was looked at with great interest. I could hear my father's name, and those of Ellenore and Count P—, whispered all round me. People stopped talking as I approached and began again as I passed on. It was clear to me that my story was being related, and no doubt each was telling it in his own way. My position was intolerable, and a cold sweat broke out on my forehead. I blushed and went white again and again.

The Baron noticed my embarrassment. He came up to me and renewed his attentions and kindnesses, took every opportunity to sing my praises, so that the power of his prestige forced the others to show me similar respect.

After they had all gone M. de T— said to me: 'I want to speak to you once again with complete frankness. Why are you willing to stay in a situation which you are finding painful? Who stands to gain by it? Do you think people don't know what is going on between you and Ellenore? Everybody knows about your bitterness and your dissatisfaction with each other. You are doing yourself harm by your weakness and no less harm by your harshness, for, to complete the illogicality of it all, you are giving no happiness to this woman who is making you so unhappy.'

I was still upset by the unpleasantness I had gone through. The Baron showed me a number of letters from my father which revealed that he was much more grieved than I had supposed. I was shaken. My irresolution was increased by the thought that I was prolonging Ellenore's sufferings. And then, as though everything were conspiring against her, in the midst of my vacillations she herself brought me to a decision by her own violence. I had been away all day, the Baron had made me stay after the reception until far into the night. In front of M. de T— I was handed a letter from Ellenore. I saw in his eyes a kind of pity for my enslavement.

Ellenore's letter was full of bitter recriminations. 'What!' I thought, 'Can't I have one single day free? Can't I breathe in peace for a single hour? She pursues me everywhere, like a slave who has to be brought back to her feet.' And, my violence increasing with my feeling of powerlessness, I went on aloud: 'Very well, I undertake to break with Ellenore. I will find the courage to tell her so myself, and you can let my father know in advance.'

As I said these words I rushed away. I felt overcome by what I had said, and only half believed in the promise I had made.

Ellenore was waiting impatiently. By a strange chance, while I had been away she had been told for the first time about M. de T——'s efforts to get me away from her. The things I had said, the jokes I had made, had all been reported to her. Once her suspicions were aroused she had linked together in her mind several circumstances which seemed to confirm them. My sudden friendship with a man I formerly never saw, and the close connexion between this man and my father seemed to her irrefutable proofs. Her anxiety had increased so rapidly in a few hours that I now found her fully convinced of what she called my perfidy.

I had reached her with my mind made up to tell her everything. But when accused by her – can you believe it? – my only concern was to avoid the whole issue. I even denied, yes denied, that day what I had decided to declare on the morrow.

It was late. I left her and hurried to bed to put an end to this long day, and when I was quite sure that it was really over I felt lightened, for the time being, of an immense burden.

On the following day I did not get up until nearly noon,

as though by putting off the beginning of our explanations I had put off the fateful moment.

Ellenore had calmed down somewhat during the night, both because she had thought things over and because of what I had said the evening before. The air of confidence with which she discussed her own affairs made it all too clear that she regarded our lives as indissolubly united. Where could I find words with which to thrust her back into solitude?

Time was flying with terrifying speed. Every minute made an explanation more imperative. Of the three days I had specified the second had already nearly gone. M. de T— expected me within two days at the very most. His letter to my father had been sent off, and I was about to break my promise without having made the slightest effort to keep it. I came and went, took Ellenore's hand, began a sentence and broke off, watched the sun on its journey down to the horizon. Night fell once again and once again I procrastinated. One day was left; one hour would be enough.

This day went by like the one before. I wrote to M. de T— asking for still more time and, as weak characters naturally do, I heaped reason upon reason in my letter to justify the delay and show that it did not in any way modify my determination, and that my connexion with Ellenore could from that very moment be regarded as broken for ever.

Chapter Ten

I FELT calmer for the next few days, having postponed indefinitely the necessity to act. This necessity no longer haunted me like a spectre and I thought I had plenty of time to prepare Ellenore. I meant to be kinder and more affectionate to her so as to preserve at any rate memories of friendship. My worry was quite different from what I had felt hitherto. I had implored Heaven for some insurmountable obstacle to come between Ellenore and me. This obstacle had now arisen and I looked upon Ellenore as a being I was about to lose. The tyranny I had so often found unbearable had ceased to have any terrors for me, for I felt freed in advance, and hence found more freedom in giving way to her still more, and felt none of that inner revolt which had formerly made me want to tear everything to pieces. All my impatience had gone, and in its place there was an unacknowledged desire to postpone the fateful moment.

Ellenore noticed that I was more affectionate and demonstrative, and she became less bitter herself. I welcomed conversations I had previously avoided and appreciated her loving words which so recently had irritated me, for now that each time might be the last they had become precious.

One evening we had separated after a more than usually delightful talk. The secret I kept locked in my heart made me sad but not excessively so. The very uncertainty of the date of the separation I had been wishing for helped to keep the thought of it out of my mind. In the middle of the night I heard an unusual noise going on in the house, but it suddenly stopped, and I dismissed it from my mind. In the morning, however, I thought about it again, and wondering what the reason was I made for Ellenore's room. To my utter astonishment I was told that for the past twelve hours she had been in a raging fever, that a doctor sent for by her servants had declared her life in danger, and that she had strictly forbidden my being informed or allowed to go to her.

I tried to insist. The doctor himself came out to impress upon me the necessity of not exciting her in any way. He did not know the reason for the order she had given, but put it down to her desire not to alarm me. I anxiously tried to find out from the servants what could have plunged her so suddenly into such a dangerous condition. After leaving me on the previous evening, I was told, she received a letter brought from Warsaw by a man on horseback, and as soon as she opened it and read it she fainted. On regaining consciousness she flung herself upon her bed and refused to utter a word. One of her maids, worried by her agitated condition, stayed in the room without her knowing, and towards midnight saw her overcome by a fit of trembling which shook the bed. The maid wanted to send for me, but Ellenore forbade this with a kind of terror so violent that nobody dared disobey. A doctor was sent for, but Ellenore refused, and was still refusing, to answer him. All night long she uttered disconnected words that nobody could understand, and often she clapped her handkerchief to her mouth as though to prevent herself from speaking.

While I was being told all this another woman who had remained near Ellenore ran out panic-stricken. Ellenore seemed to have lost the use of her senses. She could not see anything round her. Sometimes she uttered piercing screams and repeated my name; then, horrified, would make a gesture as if asking for something hateful to be kept from her.

I went in. At the foot of the bed I saw two letters. One was mine to Baron T—, the other was from him to Ellenore. The meaning of the terrible mystery was all too clear. All my efforts to gain the time I wanted for our last farewells had worked against the unhappy woman I had hoped to shield. She had read in my own hand my promises to leave her, promises dictated only by the desire to stay with her and which the very strength of that desire had made me reiterate and enlarge upon in countless ways. M. de T—'s dispassionate eye had easily read between the lines of these reiterated protestations the irresolution I was disguising and the shifts of my own uncertainty, but he had had the cruelty to calculate that Ellenore would take all that for an irrevocable decree. I went up to her. She gazed at me with unseeing eyes. I spoke to her and she shuddered. 'What is that noise?' she asked. 'It is the voice that has hurt me.' The doctor noticed that my presence was intensifying her delirium, and he urged me to withdraw. How can I describe what I went through for three long hours? At last the doctor came out. Ellenore had fallen into a heavy sleep. He did not give up hope of saving her life provided the fever had abated when she woke.

She slept for a long time. When I heard that she had awakened I wrote her a note asking her to see me. She sent a message that I could go in. I wanted to speak, but she cut me short. 'Don't let me hear a single hard word from you,' she said. 'I shall never ask for anything again, nor oppose anything; but that voice I have loved so much, that voice which used to echo in my heart, don't let it pierce my heart now. Adolphe, Adolphe, I have lacked self-control, I may have offended you, but you don't know what I have suffered, and please God you never will!'

She became extremely distressed. She put her forehead against my hand, and it felt burning hot. Her face was twisted in terrible suffering. 'In Heaven's name, listen, dearest Ellenore,' I cried. 'Yes, I am guilty; that letter ...' She shuddered and tried to move away, but I held her fast. 'In my weakness and distress,' I went on, 'I may have given in momentarily to inexorable pressure, but have you not a thousand proofs that I am incapable of wanting anything that comes between us? I have been discontented, unhappy, unfair, but possibly, by the excessive violence with which you have fought to curb my wayward imagination, you have strengthened what were only passing inclinations which I now despise. But can you question my deep affection? Are not our souls linked by countless ties that nothing can break? Is not all the past shared between us? Can we look back over the last three years and not revive impressions we have shared, pleasures we have enjoyed, troubles we have been through together? Ellenore, let us begin a new chapter this very day, let us remember the hours of joy and love.' She looked at me for some time with doubt in her eyes. 'Your father,' she said at length, 'your duties, your family, what is expected of you ...' 'Possibly,' I answered, 'some day, some time ...' But she noticed my hesitation. 'Oh, God!' she cried, 'why did he revive my hopes only to snatch them away again? Adolphe, I do thank you for your efforts, which have done me good, and all the more so because they will not cost you any sacrifice, I hope. But don't let us talk about the future, I beg of you. Don't reproach yourself, whatever happens. You have been good to me. I wanted the impossible. Love was my whole life, but it could not be yours. Now look after me for a few days longer.' The tears flowed from her eyes, her breathing became less laboured and she rested her head on my shoulder. 'This,' she said, 'is where I always wanted to die.' I held her close to my heart and once again renounced all my plans and disavowed my insensate cruelties. 'No,' she said, 'you must be free and happy.' 'How can I be if you are unhappy?' 'I shall not be unhappy for long, you will not have to go on pitying me for long.' I thrust aside fears I tried to think were illusory. 'No, no, dear Adolphe, when you have been calling upon death for a long time Heaven sends, when the hour comes, a kind of infallible presentiment warning you that your prayer is heard.' I swore I would never leave her. 'That is what I always hoped for, and now I am sure.'

It was one of those winter days when the sun seems to cast a dismal light over the greyish countryside, as though looking down in pity upon a world it has ceased to warm. Ellenore suggested we might go out. 'It is very cold,' I said. 'Never mind, I should like to go for a walk with you.' She took my arm and we went on for a long time without saying a word, she walking with difficulty and leaning heavily upon me. 'Shall we stop for a moment?' 'No,' she said, 'it is so pleasant to feel your support once again.' We relapsed into silence. The sky was clear, but the trees were bare; there was not a breath of wind and no bird cleaved the still air. Everything was motionless, and the only sound to be heard was of the frozen grass being crunched beneath our feet. 'How calm it all is!' said Ellenore. 'Look how resigned nature is! Shouldn't our hearts learn resignation too?' She sat upon a boulder, then dropped on to her knees and buried her head in her hands. I heard a few whispered words and realized she was praying. At length she rose and said: 'Let us go home. I have got cold and I am afraid of being ill. Don't say anything. I am not capable of taking it in.'

From that day onwards Ellenore was visibly weakening and fading away. I called in all the doctors I could find. Some pronounced that she was incurably stricken, others lulled me with false hopes, but nature, dark and inscrutable, carried on her inexorable work with an invisible hand. Sometimes Ellenore seemed to be recovering, and then it was as if the iron hand weighing down upon her had been lifted. She raised her drooping head, her cheeks took on a little more colour and her eyes lit up; and then suddenly the deceptive improvement was wiped out by the cruel trick of some unknown power, the cause of which no doctor's art could discover. And so I watched her slowly moving towards her end; I saw the warning signs of death stamp themselves upon her noble and expressive features. I saw, and what a humiliating and dreadful sight it was, that proud, forceful character of hers suffer a thousand confused and incoherent transformations through bodily pain as though at this awful moment her soul, crushed by her physical being, was changing its shape in countless ways in order to adapt itself the less painfully to the dissolution of her body.

One sentiment alone never varied in her, and that was her feeling for me. She was too weak to be able to say much, but she looked at me in silence and at these times I had the impression that she was begging me to give her life, which I could no longer do. I was afraid of exciting her unduly, and invented pretexts for going out, when I wandered from one to another of the places where I had been with her, weeping at the sight of stones, beneath trees, in the presence of all the things which brought back memories of her.

It was not the mere heartache of love, but a deeper and more desolate emotion, for love so identifies itself with the beloved that even in its despair there is a certain charm. Love struggles against reality, the keenness of its desire makes it overrate its strength and uplifts it in the midst of woe. But my grief was dismal and solitary. I did not hope to die with Ellenore, but was going to live on without her in the wilderness of this world, in which I had so often wanted to be an independent traveller. I had crushed the one who loved me, broken this heart which like a twin soul had been unfailingly devoted to mine in tireless affection, and already I was overcome by loneliness. Ellenore was still alive but already past sharing my confidences; I was already alone in the world and no longer living in that atmosphere of love with which she had surrounded me, and the very air I breathed seemed harsher, the faces of the men I met seemed more unconcerned. All nature seemed to be telling me that soon I should cease to be loved, and for ever.

Ellenore's peril suddenly became more imminent, and unmistakable symptoms proclaimed that her end was near. She was warned of this by a priest of her own faith. She asked me to bring her a box containing a quantity of papers, had some of them burned in her presence, but appeared to be looking for one which she could not find and was in great distress. I begged her to give up the search which was upsetting her so much and during which she fainted twice. 'Very well,' she answered, 'but, dear Adolphe, do not refuse me one request. You will find somewhere among my papers a letter addressed to you. Burn it unread, I do beseech you in the name of our love, in the name of these last moments which you have made easier for me.' I promised, and she grew calmer. 'And now leave me to devote myself to my religious duties,' she said. 'I have many sins to atone for – perhaps my love for you has been a sin, but I could not believe that if it made you happy.'

I left her and only returned with all the household for the last solemn prayers. Kneeling in a corner of the room I was part of the time lost in my own thoughts, and part, impelled by an involuntary curiosity, watching all these people gathered together, studying the terror of some and the inattention of others, and that strange effect of habit which brings indifference into all prescribed formalities and makes us regard even the most august and awe-inspiring ceremonies as matters of routine and pure form. I heard these people mechanically repeating the words of the prayers for the dying as though they themselves were never to be actors some day in a similar scene, as if they themselves were not some day to die too. And yet I was far from scorning such practices, for is there a single one of them which man in his ignorance can dare to call useless? They were bringing Ellenore some peace of mind and helping her to cross that dread threshold towards which we are all moving without being able to foresee what our feelings will then be. What surprises me is not that man needs a religion, but rather that he should ever think himself strong enough or sufficiently secure from trouble to dare reject any one of them. I think he ought, in his weakness, to call upon them all. In the dense night that surrounds us is there any gleam of light we can afford to reject? In the torrent bearing us all away is there a single branch we dare refuse to cling to?

Ellenore seemed tired after going through such a lugubrious ceremony. She sank into a quite peaceful sleep and awoke in a less troubled state. I was alone in her room, and we exchanged a few words at long intervals. The doctor whose forecasts had been most reliable had warned me that she had not twenty-four hours to live, and I looked first at a clock marking the hours and then at Ellenore's face, on which I could see no fresh change. Each passing minute revived my hopes, and I was beginning to cast doubt upon the prophecies of a perfidious art. But suddenly Ellenore leaped up in bed; I caught her in my arms. Her whole body was shaking convulsively, her eyes were searching for me, but in them was a look of vague fear, as if she were begging mercy of something threatening her but invisible to me. She sat up, then fell back, clearly trying to escape; it was as if she were wrestling with some invisible physical power which, tired of waiting for her last moment, had seized and held her in order to dispatch her on her deathbed. She finally yielded to the determined attacks of hostile nature; her body became limp. She seemed to recover some consciousness and pressed my hand. She tried to weep, but the tears would not come; she tried to speak, but her voice had gone. In resignation she dropped her head upon the arm supporting it, and her breathing became slower. A few moments later she was gone.

For a long time I remained motionless beside the dead Ellenore. The certainty of her death had not yet penetrated my soul, and my eyes stared stupidly at this inanimate body. One of her women came in and then went to spread the awful news throughout the house. The noise going on round me roused me from the lethargy into which I had sunk. I rose to my feet, and then it was that I felt the rending grief and full horror of the final farewell. All this bustling activity of daily life, all these preoccupations and comings and goings which no longer concerned her, dispelled the illusion which I was prolonging, that illusion which allowed me to believe I was still living with Ellenore. I felt the last link snap and the awful reality come between her and me for ever. How irksome this liberty now was, that I had missed so grievously! How my heart now cried out for that independence which I had often hated! Only recently all my actions had one single object; each one of them, I was convinced, would dispel some sorrow or give some pleasure. But then I complained that it should be so and felt resentful that a benevolent eye should watch over all my movements and that another's happiness should depend upon them. There was nobody to watch over my movements now, they interested nobody; there was none to dispute my comings and goings, no voice to call me back as I was going out. I was free, truly, for I was no longer loved. I was a stranger to the whole world.

All Ellenore's papers were brought to me as she had ordered. In every line I found fresh proofs of her love, new sacrifices she had made for my sake and all unknown to me. At length I found the letter I had promised to burn. At first I did not know what it was; it was unaddressed and open so a few words caught my eye in spite of myself. Try as I would not to look I could not resist the temptation to read it all. I have not the strength to copy it all out. Ellenore had written it after one of those violent scenes which had preceded her illness. 'Adolphe,' she wrote, 'why are you always against me? What crimes have I committed? Loving you and being unable to exist without you. What misguided pity makes you afraid to break a tie you find irksome and yet go on torturing the unhappy soul you remain with because of that pity? Why do you deny me the paltry satisfaction of believing you to be at any rate generous? Why do you show yourself to be so hysterical and weak? You are haunted by the vision of my grief and yet the sight of this grief cannot stop you! What is your demand? That I should leave you? Don't you see that I have not the strength? Ah, it is you, who do not love me, you who must find the strength in a heart that is weary of me and that so much love cannot touch. You will never give me that strength, but will make me languish in tears and die at your feet.'

'Tell me,' she wrote in another place, 'is there any land where I would not follow you? Any retreat where I would not stay hidden so as to be near you without being a burden? No, no, you want no such thing. Any suggestion I make in fear and trembling (for you have struck terror into me), you impatiently reject. The best I can get from you is silence. So much hardness does not go with your character. You are good, and your actions are noble and kind, but what deeds could efface the memory of your words? Those biting words echo round me; I hear them in the night, they pursue me, torture me, and poison everything you do. Must I die then, Adolphe? Very well, you shall be satisfied. She will die, this poor creature you have protected but are now hurting again and again. She will die, this wearisome Ellenore whom you cannot bear to have anywhere near you, whom you regard as an obstacle, because of whom you cannot find a single spot on this earth that does not bore you. And you will walk on alone in the midst of this crowd you are so anxious to join. You will get to know what these people really are for whose indifference you are so grateful now, and perhaps some day, when you are wounded by their stony hearts, you will miss the heart that was yours, that lived on your affection and would have braved a thousand perils in your defence, and upon which you no longer deign to bestow a single rewarding glance.'

Letter to the Publisher

Sir,

I return the manuscript you so kindly entrusted to me. I thank you for this kindness even though it has revived sad memories that time had dimmed. I knew most of the characters in this story, which is all too true. I often saw the strange and unhappy Adolphe, who is both the author and the hero; I tried to warn Ellenore – that charming woman worthy of a happier fate and a more faithful heart – against that mischievous person, no less unhappy than she, who dominated her by a kind of spell and broke her heart by his weakness. Alas, the last time I saw her I thought I had given her some strength and armed her reason against her heart. After far too long an absence I returned to the place where I had left her, to find nothing but a grave.

Sir, you should publish this anecdote. It can hurt nobody now, and in my view it might be very helpful. Ellenore's tragedy proves that even the most intense emotion cannot struggle against the accepted order of things. Society is too powerful, it has too many metamorphoses, mixes too much bitterness with any love it has not sanctioned; it favours the tendency to inconstancy, the bored impatience which are sicknesses of the soul that sometimes suddenly develop in the very midst of love. People unaffected themselves are remarkably eager to interfere in the name of morality and to hurt others by their zeal for virtue. It is as though the sight of affection were too much for them because they are incapable of it themselves, and when they can seize on an excuse they delight in attacking and destroying it. Woe betide the woman who puts her trust in a sentiment which everything conspires to poison, and against which society, once it is not obliged to respect it as legitimate, arms itself with all that is evil in the heart of man in order to discourage all that is good.

The example of Adolphe will be no less instructive if you add that after spurning the woman who loved him he was no less restless, upset, and unhappy; that he made no use of the liberty regained at the cost of so much grief and so many tears, and that by behaving in a thoroughly blameworthy manner he at the same time made himself worthy of pity.

If you want proofs of all this, Sir, read these letters which will acquaint you with Adolphe's later life. You will see him in many varied circumstances, but always the victim of the mingled selfishness and emotionalism which worked together in him for his own undoing and that of others; foreseeing the evil consequences of an act and yet doing it, and shrinking back in despair after having done it; punished for his qualities even more than for his defects because his qualities had their origin in his emotions and not in his principles; showing himself in turn the most affectionate and the most cruel of men, but as he always ended with cruelty after beginning with affection, he left no trace behind except of his misdeeds.

Reply

SIR,

Yes, I will certainly publish the manuscript you return (not that I share your view as to the service it might render; nobody in the world ever learns except at his own expense, and women who read it will all imagine they have met somebody better than Adolphe or that they themselves are better than Ellenore), but I shall publish it as a true story of the misery of the human heart. If it has any instructive lesson, that lesson is for men, for it shows that intellect, which they are so proud of, can neither find happiness nor bestow it; that character, steadfastness, fidelity, and kindness are the gifts we should pray for, and by kindness I do not mean that short-lived pity which cannot overcome impatience nor prevent it from reopening wounds which a moment of compunction had appeared to heal. The great question in life is the sorrow we cause, and the most ingenious metaphysics cannot justify a man who has broken the heart that loved him. And besides, I hate the vanity of a mind which thinks it excuses what it explains, I hate the conceit which is concerned only with itself while narrating the evil it has done, which tries to arouse pity by self-description and which, soaring indestructible among the ruins, analyses itself when it should be repenting. I hate that weakness which is always blaming others for its own impotence and which cannot see that the trouble is not in its surroundings but in itself. I might have guessed that Adolphe has since been punished for his character by his very character, that he has kept to no fixed path, adopted no useful career, that he has used up his gifts with no sense of direction beyond mere caprice, no other motive power than nervous reaction. All that, I repeat, I might have guessed even if you had not acquainted me with fresh details about his fate which I am not sure yet whether to make use of. Circumstances are quite unimportant, character is everything; in vain we break with outside things or people; we cannot break with ourselves. We change our circumstances, but we take with us into each new situation the torment we had hoped to leave behind, and as we cannot make ourselves any better by a change of scene, we simply find that we have added remorse to regrets and misdeeds to sufferings.

*A list of the most recent Penguin Classics
is given overleaf*

THE PENGUIN CLASSICS

THE MOST RECENT VOLUMES

GOWER
Confessio Amantis · *Terence Tiller*

JOINVILLE AND VILLEHARDOUIN
Chronicles of the Crusades · *M. R. B. Shaw*

EURIPIDES
Medea and Other Plays · *Philip Vellacott*

BERNAL DÍAZ
The Conquest of New Spain · *J. M. Cohen*

RACINE
Phaedra and Other Plays · *John Cairncross*

SALLUST
The Jugurthine War and The Conspiracy of Catiline · *S. A. Handford*

VOLTAIRE
Zadig and L'Ingénu · *John Butt*

LAO TZU
Tao Te Ching · *D. C. Lau*

BEAUMARCHAIS
The Barber of Seville and The Marriage of Figaro · *John Wood*

DANTE
The New Life (La Vita Nuova) · *William Anderson*

*A complete list of books is available on application to Penguin Books
whose address can be found on the back of the title page*